A Healer's Gift

Book 1 of Adventures on Brad

by

Tao Wong

Copyright

This is a work of fiction. Names, characters, businesses, places, events and incidents are either the products of the author's imagination or used in a fictitious manner. Any resemblance to actual persons, living or dead, or actual events is purely coincidental.

This book is licensed for your personal enjoyment only. This book may not be re-sold or given away to other people. If you would like to share this book with another person, please purchase an additional copy for each recipient. If you're reading this book and did not purchase it, or it was not purchased for your use only, then please return to your favorite book retailer and purchase your own copy. Thank you for respecting the hard work of this author.

Books in the
Adventures on Brad series

A Healer's Gift
An Adventurer's Heart
A Dungeon's Soul
The Arena's Call
The Adventurer's Bond
The Forest's Silence

Contents

Chapter 1

"Daniel Chai. Miner. I'm here to join the Adventurer's Guild." Answering the guard's questions, Daniel looks across the 10-foot wooden wall that separates the dungeon town of Karlak from the wilderness behind him before letting his placid brown gaze rest upon the guard and his pike once more.

The fair-haired guard, clad in a simple leather tunic and wool pants, stares at Daniel, waving his hand to summon Daniel's status screen to confirm the truth of his words. The guard reads over the information before he gestures for Daniel and his employer to enter. With a flick of the wagon's reins, Atrieus, who has sat beside Daniel during and undergone the process just moments ago himself, sets the wagon rolling.

"I turn off to the right here, boy. You okay with being paid now?" Atrieus grunts at Daniel, a hand absently coming up to scratch at his matted beard.

For a moment, Daniel is irritated but he quickly dismisses the emotion. At twenty-one, Daniel is well past the age when the term boy is appropriate, but as Atrieus has watched him grow up working the mines since he was an actual child, another thousand protests at the term are unlikely to change the old man's mind. Instead, Daniel just answers politely, "That's fine. Thank you."

"Damn waste, boy. You sure you want to do this?" Atrieus growls out, digging through the bag at his feet to pull out a small coin-laden cloth purse to hand over to Daniel.

In answering, Daniel just shakes his head, accepting his wages and waving goodbye to his temporary employer as he hops down from the ore-laden wagon. Daniel has no desire to retread that conversation either, one that has happened in many forms these past few weeks of travel. Reaching behind before the wagon leaves, he grabs his backpack and his only weapon, a 20-pound sledgehammer. Heavy as it is, Daniel carries it with little effort, muscles from years spent working the mines flexing.

After parting with Atrieus, Daniel starts off to the town center and the Adventurer's Guild, enjoying the feel of the brisk late autumn air. Home to barely more than a few thousand people, Karlak is a small town with only a single Beginner's Dungeon of ten floors. Like most dungeon towns, Karlak has grown out of the need to serve the Adventurers who bring in the majority of the town's income, and so, the entire town splays outwards from the Guild and the Dungeon entrance.

As Daniel walks deeper into town, buildings shift from simple wood to stone, prosperity showcased in architecture and materials. Around him, townsfolk weave through traffic with casual ease, most dressed in plain woolen tunics and dresses. For a town, Karlak is quite uniform in its race profile, only on occasion does Daniel spot a figure that is not human, with Beastkin the most common minority. The growth of the town has stabilized in the last few years, its presence near the contested border between Brad and the Orc nations a significant dampening factor in immigration. On the other hand, the Dungeon that provides the main source of income for the town has been around for over twenty years, and is well-mapped with a well-known and well-balanced mix of monsters, ensuring a constant stream of new hopeful Adventurers.

The latest of these hopefuls walks down the street, drawing more than a few glances his way. All new Adventurers are a potential source of income for the town, and many of the townsfolk are making quick assessments of the likelihood of his survival. His impressive musculature is a point in his favor but most quickly downgrade his chances of being a true earner. Hair so brown that it is almost black, the broad-shouldered newcomer is only 5'8" tall and human, his stature and race creating a significant disadvantage that the youngster will need to overcome.

That smells good… Daniel twists his head, searching for the aroma's origin as his stomach wakes to remind him that his last meal was early that morning. Spotting the roadside stall that has awakened his hunger, he picks up his pace before a sickening crunch followed by a chorus of screams draws his attention.

Just behind him, a child lies on the ground, his body damaged after being hit by a speeding cart. An errant wind, a loosely held flower and a hurried attempt to catch his gift are all that was required for this tragedy to happen. Unable to stop, the cart's wheels have first pushed and then rolled over the child. The child's caretaker finishes her dash out from the alleyway, a moment of distraction now twisting her face with shock and regret.

Daniel is moving without conscious thought; his worldly goods dropped behind him as he dashes to the small, crushed body. His eyes narrow as he draws upon a portion of his Gift and assesses the damage as he touches the slightly twitching body.

Shattered collarbone, crushed ribcage and heart, severe bleeding in chest cavity and stomach. Hairline cracks in the spine, a minor concussion, and a broken arm. The damage jumps out to him as he touches the child, information pouring through his mind as he catalogs and instinctively understands both the natural state of the child's body and the damage done. Information continues to flow, though he dismisses most of it from his mind. A slightly lower quantity of blood than normal, previous damage to the tendon in his ankle still a week away from healing, improper placement of the hip socket…

Even as the information comes to him, Daniel speaks familiar words, "I'm a healer. Please let me do what I can."

From the viewpoint of the child's caretaker, what Daniel does next is nothing short of miraculous. The child's caretaker is an experienced Adventurer and is well-versed in the forms of healing magic available in the world.

Nothing short of a Greater Blessing by a senior priest could have saved her nephew, and yet the stranger, without uttering a single word or calling on a God, is healing her nephew before her eyes. Bones knit, lungs inflate, and the bleeding stops within minutes. All there is to indicate that anything is even happening is the gentlest of glows coming from Daniel's hands which surround his small patient. As the glow fades, the boy's eyes open and he draws his first conscious breath before proceeding to scream and cry into his aunt's arms.

Clutching her nephew and rocking the child, the blonde-haired Adventurer looks over to Daniel who's slumped over, breathing heavily, and mouths her gratitude. Daniel just nods weakly, slowly regaining a sense of himself after the use of his Gift. As always, there is a price to pay. This time, only a half-a-day of his past - memories and lessons learnt during a fight with an overgrown badger that blocked the ore-wagons way and conversations with Atrieus - are sacrificed to his Gift.

Around Daniel, the watching crowd and the cart driver gawk at the miraculous healing; the gossip mill among the townsfolk will have new grist tonight. A good Samaritan carries over Daniel's dropped items, patting him on his back in congratulations before he leaves to finish his own errands for the day. The Samaritan's actions break the spell, with others crowding around and thanking Daniel and murmuring congratulations and consolations to the blonde-haired

Adventurer, who still clutches her nephew to her chest.

Eventually, the child calms, and the crowd disperses as Daniel's attempts to make them leave finally make a dent. Work done, he stands with a groan and bends to pick up his pack and hammer but is stopped from leaving by a hand on his arm.

"Thank you." Her voice is soft, cultured and feminine, a sharp contrast to her bearing and appearance. Short-cut yellow hair, an aquiline nose, and piercing blue eyes rest upon a face that many would call striking. The adventurer holds herself with a martial air, a hand unconsciously resting on her sword hilt, the shape of her toned and firm body easily seen under the loose cut blouse she wears. "My name is Mary Lavie, and this is Charles."

"Daniel Chai." He smiles at the boy, impulsively reaching out to ruffle the child's hair, "You'll watch yourself running out into the road next time, right?"

The boy nods slightly, his face hidden in Mary's pants. He peeks out with his own pair of blue eyes around her pant leg before burying his face once more. In the child's mind, he will still feel the breaking and the healing, a stark contrast of experiences that will, thankfully, fade in the coming hours.

As Daniel sways slightly, the Gift always taking a little of his own strength to fuel, Mary queries, "Are you okay?"

"Yes. Just a little tired and hungry. I'll be fine after a meal."

A smile brightens Mary's face, and she gestures down the road, "My sister runs the Spinning Top, just down this way. She'll want to thank you too."

For a moment, Daniel considers refusing, but he reconsiders quickly, remembering the weight of his purse. Even the payment from Atrieus is insufficient to truly fatten it out, especially with his expected expenses in the next few days. He nods gratefully in acceptance and Mary smiles, her blue eyes sparkling at his acceptance.

"This way."

Chapter 2

The Spinning Top is a typical smaller inn – at least in Daniel's limited experience. The Top is positioned close to the center of town and is made up of a mixture of wood and stone, though the inn does come with expensive blown-glass windows. The entrance of the inn leads through to a small dining room filled with rustic wooden tables and chairs flanked by a simple, worn wooden bar and a doorway to the kitchen, while a staircase opposite the entrance leads to the top floor and the rooms that the inn rents out. Like most inns in a dungeon town, it's likely the rooms can be rented on both a short and long-term basis. Daniel's musing is cut short as the smells from the kitchen set his stomach growling.

Inside, the sole worker is another tall, striking blonde woman, clad in a simple brown frock, whose matronly curves put her sister's to shame. The moment they cross the threshold of the inn, Charles squirms out from the shelter of his aunt's arms and into his shocked mother's.

"Mary…" the aghast mother and innkeeper says, bending a knee to hug her child and to survey the blood and damage. She holds Charles away from her, parsing his words while she checks him over for injury before coming to the surprising conclusion that there are none.

"We had an incident, Elise." Mary steps forward abashedly, explaining the accident in quick, concise sentences. Charles gets angry as the adults talk over him and he glares at the two, before deciding it is time to sulk. Mary flicks her hand back to Daniel, who has taken to leaning against the bar and staring into the kitchen in longing while the two sisters talk, "… and so I thought we could feed Daniel and maybe house him for a bit?"

"Jar, one plate with extra bread!" Elise calls out to the kitchen before marching over to Daniel and giving him a tight hug. "Thank you! Thank you so much!"

In a few minutes, the bustling Elise has Daniel settled and eating before she drags her bloodied child upstairs to get cleaned up. Mary takes over the counter, watching Daniel eat with a pensive look on her face, glancing between him and his hammer. It doesn't take long before Daniel is done, leaning back against the chair after mopping up the last of the stew with his bread.

That was very good. Looking around, he doesn't spot Elise to thank. He frowns slightly, impatient to complete his task but unwilling to leave without thanking her for the meal. As he debates what to do, his thoughts are interrupted by Mary.

"Are you going to join the Guild?" she asks, nodding to his hammer. The guess was not hard since the vast majority of fit young men coming into town had only one goal. She purses her lips as he acknowledges her question with a nod. "And that's your weapon?"

"Why? Is it a problem?" Defensive, Daniel places his hand on the hilt of the hammer.

"It is. It's too big and unwieldy for a dungeon." As he opens his mouth to reply, Mary raises her hand and forestalls him, continuing, "I'm sure you used it while traveling here. Probably killed a few monsters too. There's no arguing that it's a fearsome weapon.

"But you have to land your blow. You need space to swing it and time to recover after you've swung. In a dungeon where you might face two or three different monsters at the same time, often faster and smaller than you, it won't work."

Daniel grunts, hunching slightly at each of her words. He knows it is not perfect; it's not as if he hadn't experienced much of what she said himself. "It's what I have."

His words are not unexpected, and as soon as they leave his mouth, Mary turns to the staircase, calling upwards, "Elise, we're going out. I'll bring him back later! Jar, put his bags in room 3!"

The blonde stands swiftly, pushing her chair back into place before walking to the exit. When she notices Daniel is not moving, she barks out a single word. "Come."

"Umm… what's going on?" Hurrying to catch up with her, Daniel stumbles along, trying to gauge their destination in this strange city. Even as they hurry, human townsfolk offer Mary a quick smile and greeting, each acknowledged by Mary with a short nod.

"We're going to the Guild to get you registered. You do have the twenty silver, correct?" She doesn't acknowledge his hasty nod, continuing to speak even as she strides along.

"After that, we'll get you the training you need to wield a proper weapon."

"Training! I can't afford that!" Daniel exclaims, catching up with her and trying to slow her down to speak.

"Who asked you to pay?" Arriving at the doors of the Adventurer's Guild, she strides in and heads to the nearest empty counter. An attendant walks over unhurriedly, tall and thin with a full mop of curly black hair. He smiles slightly as he spots the harried Daniel behind Mary before focusing on her entirely.

"What can I do for you, Mary?" The attendant smiles, his face wrinkling and adding to its lines as he runs a hand through his hair to bring some order to it.

"Got a newbie who needs to be registered, Liev." She gestures behind, indicating Daniel who's staring around in confusion. Liev smiles placatingly at the young man, pulling some papers and a small crystal ball out from beneath the counter.

"Not a problem. Just put your hand here; don't be shy." Smiling encouragingly, Liev has Daniel place his hand on the crystal ball while he coaches out the information that he needs to finish the registration. "Good, good. A Level 7 Miner. Ooh, very good, a Minor Healing spell. Yes, we can definitely register you as an Adventurer."

At the end of his words, a low azure light glows on the crystal bringing another contented smile to Liev's face. "And done. That'll be twenty silver."

As Daniel finishes paying, he can't help but wonder if all his dreams have come true already. Another barked command to follow pulls him out of his contemplation as he hurries to catch up with the impatient Mary as she strides out of the Guild house. While he rushes after her, he calls up his Status Screen to marvel at his new position.

Name: Daniel Chai
Class: Level 1 Adventurer (0%)
Sub-classes: Level 7 (Miner) (14%)
Human (Male)

Statistics
Life: 164
Stamina: 164
Mana: 129
Critical Hit Chance: 4%

Attributes
Strength: 17
Agility: 12
Constitution: 23
Intelligence: 14
Willpower: 16
Luck: 13

Skills
Unarmed Combat: Level 2 (47/100)
Clubs: Level 3 (21/100)

Perception: Level 3 (21/100)
Mining: Level 7 (78/100)
Healing: Level 5 (84/100)
Herb Lore: Level 3 (31/100)
Cooking: Level 2 (37/100)
Singing: Level 2 (14/100)

Skill Proficiencies
Mapping (II)

Spells
Minor Healing (I)

Gifts
Martyr's Touch - The caster may heal oneself or others by touch and concentration, sacrificing a portion of his life to do so. Cost varies depending on the extent of the injuries healed.

It's a surprise for Daniel when Mary finally comes to a stop and thrusts a shield and mace at him. He reaches out and grabs the items automatically and then frowns, dismissing the Status Screen to pay proper attention to what he has been given. The mace is a simple construct, though instead of metal, its top is padded with wood and wrapped in cloth. A training weapon, though of better quality than he's ever wielded before. The shield is a simple wooden shield banded with iron around the corners and weighted with extra lead at the back.

He pauses, looking at the weapons in his hand before looking up and around himself for the first time. Although the training hall they are standing in is made of stone, its high ceiling is vaulted with wooden beams. Windows are thrown open to bring in fresh air, but where wall space is available, weapon racks full of training gear hang. The ground beneath his feet is hard-packed soil, though in the corner he notices a rougher training ground. All around him, adventurers, and those who wish to be adventurers, train.

"Mary…"

"Litzburn!" Mary ignores Daniel again, waving to a towering, bald, ebony-skinned man who seems to be in command of the training floor. The man strides up to them, smiling widely at Mary and then nodding in acknowledgment as she speaks. "This is Daniel. He's joining today."

Litzburn chuckles as Daniel opens his mouth to protest to Mary's already departing back. He drops a surprisingly delicate hand onto the new Adventurer's shoulder and gently but firmly guides Daniel onto the training floor, "Don't bother, kid; she isn't listening. Now, follow along, you'll want to know this."

Chapter 3

Hours later, Daniel lies on his back groaning in pain, unwilling to move another inch and feeling thankful that he's not training in the heat of summer. He hasn't felt this tired in years, not since his first year as a miner. For hours, he has been put through various exercises. Firstly, basic fitness tests and weight carrying before moving on to more intricate martial forms with both mace and shield. Once he had spent fifteen minutes working with his new training equipment, Litzburn had walked over and ordered the young man to return the set that he had been working with to the walls, before providing him with even heavier equipment.

Hours of drills then came, at first beginning with simple actions such as stepping and striking before evolving into more and more complicated sequences as Litzburn realises Daniel isn't a complete novice. Every time Daniel flags, Litzburn is at his side, barking at him to pick it up and move faster, driving the young man on. Still, he can't complain as he stares at the blue notification window floating in front of his eyes.

Skill Increase
Clubs: Level 3 (27/100) +3

He's interrupted in his thoughts by a shadow falling over his still form and a booted foot prodding him. He turns his head to meet the gaze of his smiling tormentor. "You did well today.

Litzburn tells me you have good stamina and some adequate training for a beginner."

"Thanks…" Daniel mutters before pulling himself up from the ground shakily. Normally he'd heal himself slightly with his gift, just enough to take away the fatigue to let him work more but after this morning's events, he decides against it. Enough has already been lost for one day.

"Come on. We're heading back to the Top. Tomorrow, Litzburn will have you work with some of the other students, and I'll train with you in the evening." Mary is already walking off, and the bemused Daniel follows along, accepting that the young lady doesn't seem to have any desire to waste time.

"Mary, thank you for the training. But, don't we have to pay or something?" Catching up, Daniel gestures back to the training grounds that they have just left.

Mary snorts, before she stops, realising that, of course, Daniel wouldn't know, "I own these training grounds. Well, my sister and I do," she corrects herself, before continuing, "Litzburn is the Master-at-Arms my father hired before he died and while Litzburn might run it, we do own it."

"Oh." Pondering the news for a moment, Daniel continues, "Is that where you learnt to fight too?"

A nod confirms his guess which makes Daniel fall silent, a part of him considering how strong Mary might actually be. She moves with a fluid grace, every action like a part of a dance. Perhaps he too could learn some of that?

It takes them only a few minutes to reach the Top, where Elise seems to have been joined by a pair of waitresses. Spotting her sister, Elise waves them over before directing Daniel to a seat and placing a tankard of beer and an evening meal in front of the weary youngster. The heavenly smell of roast lamb with vegetables and mashed potatoes is all the enticement Daniel needs to throw himself at the meal with gusto. Leaving the young man to eat, Elise drags her sister off and begins a furious conversation with her.

Daniel digs into the meal, casting an occasional curious glance at the arguing pair, but after a moment, he dismisses it. Best not to get involved in a family fight. Instead, he spends his time eating and surveying the various other customers, many of whom look to be guards and adventurers. Each group sits with others of their kind, clustered in tables and partaking of the food with relish. Daniel is so caught up in people watching that it's a surprise when Elise speaks to him, "I know it's been a hectic day, Daniel, but you really should have stayed for me to say thank you properly."

"I'm sorry," Daniel tries to explain. "Mary dragged me off and then…"

"I know." She gestures with the dirty washcloth in her hand. "She told me. She says she'll be teaching you for the rest of the week before you go into the Dungeon. Good."

"About that...." Daniel opens his mouth, wanting to protest about being given free room and board.

"Daniel, you saved my son's life. The least we can do is increase your chances of surviving in the Dungeon." She suddenly snorts, shaking her head, the long-time resident of a dungeon town adding her two cents, "I don't believe you intended to use that hammer in there. You won't make it past the second floor with that thing."

"Come on, it's not that bad!" protests Daniel.

"Yes, it is. I've lived here all my life and let me tell you, Daniel, one in four Adventurers die on their first foray into a Beginner Dungeon. Of those that make it past the first zone, only one in ten ever completes the Dungeon. Being an Adventurer is dangerous." As she speaks, Elise holds Daniel's gaze. Though she is telling the truth, what Elise leaves out is that many Adventurers do not complete the Dungeon by choice. There are significant riches to be made continuously 'farming' the dungeon monsters for their mana crystals and other dropped items. Riches that an experienced Adventurer could gain with minimal risk.

"That bad?' Daniel's eyes widen, completely taken in by Elise. For a moment, doubt creeps in, and he second guesses his new future and his decision to travel, to adventure, to be his own man. It is a brief moment of hesitation that is soon pushed aside as Daniel refuses to give up before he has even begun. "Thank you. For the advice and the room. And thank Mary for the training."

Satisfied that she has won, Elise bestows a kindly smile on Daniel before she hurries off to care for her patrons. Left alone, Daniel makes his way to his assigned room to wipe himself down and rest. It has been a long day, and tomorrow Litzburn has promised that the real training will begin.

Chapter 4

In the morning, a hurried breakfast is all that Daniel has time for before he rushes over to the training hall. Litzburn is already waiting and directs Daniel to join the other trainees in a slow warmup jog around the hall. The remainder of the day falls into the pattern of the previous day – calisthenics and weight training for a few hours before they dive into the meat of the program, focusing on the use of his mace and shield. Outside of a short lunch break, Daniel is given very little time to rest, which makes him truly grateful for the packed lunch that was pressed on him by Elise as he left that morning.

By the time late afternoon has come, Daniel is beaten and ragged. Numerous other trainees have come and gone throughout the day, most only spending only a few hours in the hall before leaving to run other tasks. Only a few trainees stay throughout the day, each of these is given extra special attention by Litzburn for their dedication. Daniel is focused on a paired movement and striking exercise, attempting to keep his feet, shield and mace moving together and so he never notices Mary's entrance and silent consideration.

"Hold!"

Caught in the middle of a swing, his opponent freezes and steps back, putting distance between himself and Daniel. Daniel freezes too, his shield half-raised to block the blow, his mace swinging from below in return and paused too.

Daniel stands there, frozen for a moment before he remembers to step away from his opponent as well, ensuring a safe distance is created. Only then does he look over to Litzburn who is gesturing him over to where he and Mary stand.

"Take a ten-minute break. Then you'll be sparring with Mary," Litzburn calls out to Daniel as he nears before turning away from the tired young man and walking over to address the rest of his students.

Stifling a groan, Daniel flops down in the corner of the training floor before reminding himself to grab a drink of water. As he rests, he stares at his newly updated skill screen, the second one to appear after his rests.

Skill Increase
Clubs (Basic): 37/100 (+3)

Skill Increase
Shields (Basic): 11/100 (+5)

I'm learning very fast, muses Daniel as he dismisses the skill screen. *I guess that's what a real trainer and training ground will do.*

Even to his untrained senses, Daniel can sense the Skill stones that dot the building, helping him to learn faster, even while Litzburn corrects his mistakes with a critical, experienced eye. Still, he can feel a wave of apprehension rising in him at the thought of actually sparring with Mary. He could tell that she was going to be significantly more experienced.

Damn it. Stop worrying. She isn't going to hurt you. Drink some more water and let's get going. Chiding himself, Daniel pushes himself up and walks over the water barrel again before approaching the waiting senior Adventurer.

Mary's dressed in a near replica of her clothing from yesterday - a simple white blouse with a black lace vest and tight, brown pants that show off her trim body. Her sword is strapped to her right side, still sheathed, and in her left hand, she holds a training sword. She looks Daniel over critically, her bright blue eyes clinical in their assessment before she waves him onto the training floor, before following along behind.

A brief salute is exchanged, and immediately, Daniel hunkers down beneath his shield, his mace at his side near his waist as he circles her probing for an opening. Mary turns, only shifting her blade slightly to cover the exposed angles until Daniel lunges forward, committing to an attack. With the barest of motions, the attack is deflected, and Mary returns a riposte aimed at Daniel's shoulder which he barely dodges by jumping back. Regaining his footing, Daniel hunkers back down and works to calm his nerves, the barely moving form of Mary an intimidating presence. Again, he begins to move forward, this time attempting a blow from over his shield. Mary catches his mace in a casual block, and as he recovers, she casually strikes him on his upper arm.

He growls, trying another attack which is just as quickly and neatly defended before her words ring out, "Stop leaning in before each attack."

The sparring continues for an hour with short breaks as she corrects his form and attacks. Not once does he even come close to landing a blow on her, each attack nonchalantly deflected with a flick of a wrist or twist of the elbow. After each committed attack, Mary launches a single return blow of her own, forcing Daniel to scramble to block or dodge in turn.

"Hold!" she says. Daniel pauses and steps back, ensuring he is safe from a return attack before lowering his tired arms.

"Good. We're done. We'll work on what we talked about tomorrow. I'll see you for dinner at the Top." With that and a final salute, Mary turns and strides out of the training ground. Daniel sighs, watching her go and feels somewhat inadequate at his failure to land a single blow. Before he can begin to get too morose, a hand lands on his shoulder.

"Don't worry about it. Even experienced Adventurers had a hard time landing a hit on her — and that was before she first entered the Dungeon and leveled up. That girl, her ability, it isn't normal. You did well for your first time." Chuckling, Litzburn pushes Daniel towards the racks. "Best get dressed and moving; she hates to be kept waiting."

***

At the Spinning Top, Mary waves Daniel over to her table where a meal is already set, awaiting him. Taking a seat gratefully, Daniel speaks, "Ummm… so, thank you for today."

"It's fine. Now, eat. You need it." She waves him towards the food before she continues. "What do you know about the Dungeon in Karlak?"

Caught between two conflicting orders, Daniel chews quickly and swallows before answering. "It's a Beginner Dungeon, so it's suitable for those just starting out Adventuring. There are ten levels, with the monsters growing stronger at each level. The Dungeon is considered extremely suitable for melee fighters starting out and… umm…. that's about it."

"So, nothing really. Do you know what kind of Dungeon this is? What monsters spawn in the first sector? Do you even know about sectors? How about how many mobs you can expect to see per level? Who is the Dungeon boss? What kind of weaponry is most suitable? Why are melee fighters most suited for this dungeon?" Mary fires question after question at Daniel, waving her own fork as she speaks.

Daniel stops chewing at her words, hunching a bit into his chair as he realises exactly how unprepared he is. Seeing his reaction, Mary relents a little.

"It's fine. It's just a typical beginner's mistake. Just, do your research next time, alright?" Mary waits for Daniel's sheepish nod before leaning forwards and meeting his eyes, "Melee fighters have a bad enough reputation for never using our heads. There's no reason to foster that reputation further. Prior research about a Dungeon is what separates the professionals from the dead."

Pausing to emphasise her point, and making sure it sinks home, she continues to answer her own questions, "It's common knowledge that Dungeons are a way for Erlis to cleanse herself of the corruption that Ba'al releases into the mana flows. The monsters created in a Dungeon are patterned upon the various minions of Ba'al, though they do not truly 'live'. It's why they do not often exit the Dungeons and when they do, most break down in short order. Of course, a Dungeon that isn't regularly cleared of monsters will have no choice but to strengthen those monsters, eventually giving them sufficient strength to leave the Dungeon itself. In time, an unchecked Dungeon can become the source of Ba'al's infestation, leading to tragedies like the Abandoned Lands. Of course, as Adventurers, we're mostly concerned about the mana crystals — the seed that Erlis uses to create the monsters and our main source of income.

"There are two kinds of Dungeons - the permanent Dungeons like the ones in Karlak and the capital Warbis, and then the temporary Dungeons which randomly appear. Permanent Dungeons rarely change their overall structure, often fixing their floors and the monsters for years at a time. While minor changes in designs and traps do occur, the overall structure of a permanent Dungeon stays the same and, as such, they are often considered 'safer' than temporary Dungeons.

"Temporary Dungeons, or instances, are rare. They appear in places where mana and Ba'al's corruption have built up and by their very nature, are extremely chaotic. Monsters and layouts may change significantly from one trip to the next which make them extremely dangerous to clear. However, because they are built from corrupt mana sources that have temporarily congregated, these Dungeons often do not last longer than a few completions."

Having finished his meal, Daniel places his utensils down and stays silent, listening to the lecture. It is pleasant to not move, and the information she provides is important, even if some of it is well known. Seated, Daniel can feel his body recovering already, regaining the strength it lost through the day.

"Now, for ease of understanding, the Adventurer's Guild has split each Dungeon into sectors - a sector ranging from a single floor to ten. Sectors are grouped due to the nature of the monsters, the traps and the layouts of the floors. At the end of each sector, it's possible that there are sector bosses - monsters whose strength is significantly greater than the average mob already encountered. They aren't even necessarily a similar monster to those that you have met on that floor, though most Dungeons keep to a theme of some form. Though this isn't always true, it is in the case of Karlak.

"In Karlak, there are three sectors which consist of three floors. The tenth floor isn't a true 'floor', but a single room with the Final Boss monster of the Dungeon. The first sector in the Karlak Dungeon is inhabited by Kobolds. They move in groups with a maximum of three Kobolds at the third level, but for the first level you'll at most run into two of them, and even then, that's highly unlikely."

She pauses for a moment, taking a drink from her tankard and Daniel takes the moment to ask a question, "What are they like?"

"Kobolds?" For a moment Mary racks her brains, trying to recall the looks of the creature. It has been many years since she has fought one of those herself. "Small – about three to four feet tall at most. Extremely thin, very fast with elongated ears and pale grey skin from living underground for so long. They rarely wear much in terms of armour and in the first level wield a dagger-like item, though some carry slings for ranged attacks. Overall, they are the perfect mob for beginner melee fighters."

Daniel nods in thanks, and seeing he has no further questions Mary continues, "Due to the prevalence of the Kobolds in the first few levels, corridors are small and cramped in many areas. There are numerous side-tunnels in the first few levels with no safe zones for healing. Large weapons like a spear or hammer," she flashes him a quick smile at that one before continuing, "are not advisable due to the lack of room. All adventurers should carry a backup dagger for close combat fighting due to the layout, and they should expect potential sneak attacks at all times."

Opening her mouth to continue her lecture, she's interrupted by her sister, Elise, who is accompanied by a young boy clad in a ragged tunic who could at best be eight years old. "Sorry about this, Mary, but young Pierson needs to speak with Daniel."

The young boy impatiently pushes forward, placing a hand on Daniel's arm, "Sir, Charles mentioned you healed him. Healed him good when he was hurt." At Daniel's nod, he rushes on, "Please, will you come and heal my mum?"

Chapter 5

Following Pierson through the lightly illuminated streets of Karlak, Daniel is struck by the thought that this is his first foray into the town at night. Old tales about the dangers of the city make Daniel's hand open and close in want of his hammer. Unknown to him, Karlak is actually a very safe town as guards routinely patrol the streets looking for trouble. Regular troublemakers were sentenced to work in the Dungeon, collecting a set number of mana stones before they were released. Troublemakers and thieves would either die in the Dungeon or just became Adventurers after their term was done since the work was easier and more regular than anything they could do on the outside.

Unfortunately, Daniel knows none of this, and he continually twists his head around, peering into the shadows of alleyways and doorways as they pass expecting to be robbed. It is only Pierson's words that distract him from his obsession. "You can heal my mum, right, Sir? Please?"

"I'll do my best," Daniel hesitantly promises, knowing that even his Gift has limits. Not many for sure, but the cost did increase. Still, the conversation does take his mind away from the supposed dangers of the night as they leave the center of town.

"Charles said you brought him back alive. My mum's not dead. So you can heal her," the child continues, pulling on Daniel's hand to hurry him along.

"He wasn't dead…" realising he forgot the child's name, Daniel trails off. Instead, he changes the subject before Pierson can continue. "Are we heading to your home?"

"No. We're going to the Clinic!"

Even Daniel can hear the capitalization in the child's voice, forcing him to enquire, "The Clinic?"

"Yeah, that's where we all go. The poor. Kyra treats us all." Pierson happily imparts his knowledge to the adult. "She's real pretty, but she never lets me eat any sweets. And she said she couldn't help my mum… but you can! So you're better."

"Kid…" Daniel trails off, shaking his head. No use trying to dissuade him and destroying the child's hope just yet. Instead, he asks another question. "Who's Kyra? Is she a healer?"

"Yeah, the best. Well, other than you. Mum says she opened a clinic years ago and since then, she treats everyone, even if you're poor. She never says no, but it's boring going because there's always people there," Pierson explains.

Much of the information imparted by Pierson isn't particularly surprising to Daniel. Healing potions and spells were expensive as materials, and experienced users were rare. Healers rarely ventured into Dungeons to gain experience faster which meant they could only increase levels by practising their craft. Unfortunately, most skills had diminishing returns in their experience gain if the same action was taken over and over again — which of course was what healers mostly did. There really wasn't anything new to be learnt, dealing with the common cold for the hundredth time. Powerful healing spells drained mana at a significant rate, and with individual mana pools taking up to eight hours to refill, common folk rarely had access to powerful healing magics.

The rarity of healers is one reason Miles, the mine overseer, and many of his miner colleagues had tried to convince him to stay at the mining camp, or at the very least, to not waste his Gift and train to become a healer. Daniel's healing Gift was rare and powerful, especially since it drew upon his experience and energy and thus was a source of energy separate from his mana. Daniel could have become a truly miraculous healer, able to heal using two forms of energy - along with more mundane skills. Even the Royal Healer was known to do very little actual magic-assisted healing since he would need to husband his mana in case of a sudden need for his abilities.

Still, the fact that there is a location in Karlak where the poor can find some form of healing, overworked and crowded as it might be, is a surprise. Daniel can't help but wonder what kind of person this Kyra was. All idle thoughts come to an end as they finally arrive at the Clinic. A weather-worn sign hangs outside with the universal symbol of healing, a crossed pair of hands with jagged lines coming from the hands to indicate an aura. The two-story building itself sprawls across two lots and is by far the best-kept building in the neighborhood with fully working windows and doorways, even if obvious signs of wear and patching are visible.

Pierson doesn't even pause before pushing open the door and is closely followed by Daniel. Inside, what looks to be a waiting room is filled with the poorer denizens of Karlak awaiting treatment. Few even bother looking up from their seats as the child and Daniel enter, lost in their thoughts as they are. Ailments range from simple open wounds that need stitching and broken bones to the disease ridden. Pierson doesn't spare a glance to those inside, instead rushing to the corridor behind and leading Daniel up the stairs to a second-floor room.

In the room, a surprisingly young woman lies, wasting away. Pierson's mother's face is drawn, any excess fat removed, and what would have been once a beautiful face is drawn in pain. Through the room, an obnoxious stench of puss and other unmentionables permeates, making Daniel gag at the stench.

"Mum, I brought him. You'll be fine. He'll heal you." Pierson's voice comes to Daniel as he walks over, a hand landing on the young woman's shoulder so that he may activate his Gift.

Oh, so that's what it looks like when it's advanced. None of the men I treated at camp ever let it get that far before they saw me. His eyes locked on her groin area as he followed the lines of infection spreading outwards and invading her body. He senses the raised temperature, body struggling to fight off the infection and failing. *She will be dead in a few days if I do nothing.*

"Why are you waiting? Come on. Heal her." Almost stamping his feet in impatience, Pierson pushes at Daniel's leg. Then, a trace of fear crosses his voice as he realises where the young Adventurer is looking, the young child's voice beginning to tremble, "You aren't not going to heal her are you? Because she's a… a… whore?"

Shaken by the child's voice, Daniel pulls himself away from the mother to look at Pierson. "It's not that, kid. I just needed to know what I was healing first. My magic isn't like the others… I need to understand what I'm going to fix before I can do it."

She's too weak to use her own energy. We have to drop her temperature first then we can cleanse the infection from her body. After that, we'll have to seal the wounds, so she's not re-infected. Exhaling forcefully, Daniel reaches out to place his hand on the delirious woman's head as he kneels down. "Pierson, this is going to take a while. So don't worry if nothing seems to be happening, I'm going to have to go slow with your mum."

As he finishes speaking, Daniel calls forth his Gift and sends it into her, easing his energy just a little bit into her body at a time. He pushes it slowly, letting it fill her body without attempting to guide it at all at first, the energy lighting up along the meridian pathways of her body starting from her head downwards. As his energy fills her, her breathing eases, and her heartbeat steadies under the passive influence of his Gift. When he is ready, finally, he begins to actively manipulate the energy, working to lower her over-heated body before beginning the long, slow process of flushing her body of the toxins that permeate her blood and the infection that causes it.

The healing isn't easy; each moment a sacrifice. He doesn't speak of the cost of using his Gift to others, though his grandfather and a few others have guessed long ago. In Brad, the Gifted were believed to be blessed by Erlis herself, in others they were considered curses laid by Ba'al for the toll each Gift took upon their users. In truth, none knew where the Gift came from. Like all Gifts, Daniel's had a cost and his tore away knowledge and experience with each moment of use. Knowledge of past actions, past conversations, training and experience drawn from his body.

Hours later, Daniel opens his eyes and tries to stand, pushing against the bedframe. Legs locked in a single position for hours are unable to hold the weight placed on them, and Daniel stumbles forward, caught from crashing into his patient by a steadying hand.

"Thank you," Daniel croaks out as he sways slightly. He is quickly guided to a seat by his unexpected helper, a matronly older lady.

"No, thank you. Peony would be dead without you." The old lady guides him to a waiting seat before turning back to her task of wiping down the patient. It's only then that he realises how much worse the room smells now.

All the toxins and infection from Peony's body have leaked into the room, creating a truly horrendous stench that not even an open window can aid.

"I do hope all your work isn't as smelly as this," the old lady continues as she bathes the newly-healed young woman.

Daniel grins weakly before quenching his thirst with a glass of water. It's been ages since he used so much power on a single individual, even Charles's healing was simpler than eradicating the disease that had ravaged Peony's body. Still, he cannot help but smile as he watches the young woman rest easier, Pierson curled up at the base of her bed asleep. As he contemplates his work, another figure strides in, one that causes his jaw to drop. An elf!

Never having seen an elf before in real life, Daniel stares at the elf with undisguised awe. The elf is tall, clad in a simple green frock that hugs her slim upper body on top of a buxom chest, waist-length blonde hair spilling out behind long pointed ears. The elf moves with a lithe grace over to Pierson's mum, a delicate hand moving in arcane gestures as she checks on the condition of the patient. Satisfied, the blonde elf turns to Daniel who has managed to close his mouth at last and stand up.

"I'm Daniel. Would you be Kyra?" He offers his hand to shake which is promptly taken. Her skin is surprisingly soft and smooth, a sharp contrast to his own rough and calloused hands.

"Khy'ra," she corrects his pronunciation off-handedly, not expecting him to get it right as she turns to point at Pierson's mum. "Your Gift, it's incredible. It's at least the equivalent of a Tier 4 Healing Spell, maybe 5. Are you able to use it again today?"

"Kind of. That took a lot out of me…" as he speaks, he meets the enthusiastically nodding Khy'ra's gaze. Sparkling green eyes meet his own, and Daniel's excuses catch in his suddenly dry mouth. "Maybe a bit."

"Good. I'm not much of a healer; I only know a single Tier 3 spell so there's much that I cannot do for these people. There are a few others I'd love you to see if you are willing?" She casts an entreating look at Daniel who sighs, consoling himself that he will get to spend more time with the beautiful creature before him.

"I'll do what I can."

"Excellent!" Gripping his arm to her full chest, Khy'ra drags Daniel out of the room to visit her patients, already beginning to list the many issues that they face. Behind them, the matronly old woman is left alone, smiling slightly at the departing smitten young man.

Chapter 6

The following days for Daniel each fall into the same pattern as the day before. An early breakfast in the Top followed by training with Litzburn at the hall. In the late afternoon, Daniel spars with Mary before retiring for dinner with her and a lecture about the basics of Adventuring. The moment dinner is over, he is escorted by a grateful Pierson to the Clinic where he works alongside the minimal staff, using his healing skills, spells and on occasion, his Gift to reduce the waiting line. The line at the Clinic never seems to reduce, no matter how much he does, but the work itself is rewarding.

Each day is packed, every morning a struggle as Litzburn berates him for forgetting part of what he learnt the day before, driving the willing Adventurer ever harder. On the fourth day of training, he finally manages to make Mary move from her spot, the casual blocks insufficient. On the sixth, after chaining together a series of strikes, he makes her move regularly and pick up speed. On the seventh day, he finally breaks through.

Level Up!
Adventurer Level 2
You have gained 5 attribute points and 1 skill proficiencies.

The Level Up notification is dismissed, leaving Daniel on the floor rubbing his jaw. The level up had caught him unawares, distracting him for a crucial moment leading to the blow that he forgets to block properly. Still, he can't help smiling. Sure, the first level was always easier to gain after any class change, but in a week!

Mary stands over Daniel, offering him a hand up and a murmur of, "Congratulations."

"Thank you. You and Litzburn. This, this will help a lot," Daniel says as he lets himself get pulled up.

"It's your hard work." Mary smiles, clapping him on the back. "We're done for today. You might be rather useless in the mornings from what Litzburn says, but you work hard. You should spend the evening deciding where to put your points. I have dinner with Elise and Charles tonight as I leave tomorrow."

Daniel nods, a bit impatient to review his Status Screen. It's been such a busy week, he hasn't had time to review it, but he can certainly see the wisdom of her words. After all, he's going into the Dungeon tomorrow for the first time. "Thank you again."

"Daniel, your Gift – don't take it for granted. Most others have to start out slow, buying potions from the apothecary for healing and if they run out or are too gravely injured, leave the Dungeon until they are healed. You don't have to. It's also a double-edged sword as you may come to rely on it too much. Just, don't push yourself too hard. That includes the Clinic," Mary adds. She hasn't asked what his Gift costs him as yet, but it was common knowledge that there must be a cost of some form. Still, his performance in the morning has given her an inkling, but it was his secret to keep. As they talk, Mary leads him to the corner where she hands over her training sword to be put away once again. The clerk returns after setting her training sword in its special spot in the armory with a real mace which she takes from him with a nod. Mary then turns to Daniel, offering him the mace. "This is the last thing I can do for you for now Daniel. The rest will be up to you."

Daniel takes it and murmurs his gratitude, hefting the mace and looking it over.

Steel Mace
Damage: 3 - 7 + .5 Strength + 2 Quality Bonus
Durability: 50/50
Item Class: Common
Quality: Good (+2 bonus to damage)

Daniel can't help but marvel at the weapon, the nicest he has ever owned before eventually slipping the mace through a loop in his belt, "I talked to Khy'ra last night. I'll visit once in a while, but I won't be there every day anymore. As much as I like helping, I can't. She understands. Mary, all this - the training, the mace, the advice, how can I ever thank you?"

"You don't need to. I'm leaving tomorrow for Starhaven. My team's waiting for me, and I need to get back. If you are ever in Starhaven, buy me a drink as thanks if you must. Just don't come too fast." Mary smiles slightly at that, clapping him on the shoulder once more before turning to leave. Daniel understands her message - Starhaven only has Expert level Dungeons and was no place for a novice Adventurer like him. Not yet, at least.

***

That evening, after a rushed dinner by himself, Daniel lies in bed and debates what to do with his new attribute points and skill proficiencies.

5 attribute points and 1 skill proficiency to allocate. Unlike his previous class as a Miner, the Adventurer class was much more open-ended on its attribute point allocation. Strength, Agility and Constitution were all key to his needs as a melee fighter, but it was his Intelligence and Willpower that dictated his ability to heal. He frowns for a moment, deciding to put a couple of extra points into Agility and a point each into Constitution, Intelligence and Wisdom. He was more than strong enough for now.

That done, he calls up his skill proficiency tree and stares at the new options available for him. All that training has increased his skills in both Shield, Dodge, Combat Sense and Club offering him more options than he knew what to do with. As he gains ability in each skill, new skill proficiencies would become available that allowed him to enhance the basic abilities of each skill. This even translated to his healing skill, with both mundane options like First Aid or at higher levels, powerful healing spells. Unsure of what to do, Daniel decides to peruse his proficiencies again, musing over his options.

An upgrade to his Minor Healing Spell would reduce the mana cost and increase the amount healed slightly. It was a good option for both the Clinic and the Dungeon. However, he had the backup of his own Gift which should be enough for now, so he dismisses that option.

In terms of defense, he could learn Hard Block, offering him a chance to beat aside an opponent's weapon and potentially riposte on the line of attack. A truly successful hard block could even damage or disarm an opponent. On the other hand, Tumbling under Dodge would provide a more efficient means of getting out of the way of large attacks or groups, though Sway was a passive skill proficiency that would offer him the chance to dodge blows by inches without giving ground. Daniel knew Mary favored that option, allowing her to hold her ground even against the strongest opponents. Sway was a skill particularly useful for the smaller, lighter Adventurer but after consideration, Daniel discards it. It just doesn't suit his fighting style, especially as he intends to specialise in the use of a shield when he could afford one.

Dueling from Combat Sense would give him a bonus to hit and his critical hit skill while fighting a single opponent but as he was a solo Adventurer, multiple mobs were a guarantee at some point. While Daniel has no shield or armour to his name at this time, he has more hit points than most beginning Adventurers since he started out his career later than most of them. Trusting in his ability to take damage, Daniel dismisses all but his combat skill proficiencies to review.

Shield Bash

An attack with your shield, turning it into an offensive weapon as well as a defensive tool.
Skill: Active
Cost: 12 Stamina
Effect: User's Bash does 1-2 points of damage + 0.5 per level of the Shield Skill. Has a 1% chance per level of Shield Skill chance to Stun for 5 seconds.

Power Strike

Powerful single strike that causes additional damage to an opponent.
Skill: Active
Cost: 15 Stamina
Effect: User's Power strike does 50% more damage + 2% per level of Club skill.

Double Strike

Cross strike allows the wielder to launch a chained attack, striking twice in the time it would take an inexperienced attacker to attack once. Each strike (if it lands) is at 70% of the damage.
Skill: Active
Cost: 25 Stamina

Effect: User strikes twice in quick succession. Each strike does 70% of normal damage. Damage increases +0.5% per Club skill level of user.

Power Strike was a very common attack for most melee fighters. It provided a high level of damage and could crush many lower level enemies if he could increase his skill level with clubs sufficiently. Shield Bash was probably the next most common attack form, a safe skill that made both hands dangerous and one that was favored by shield users like himself. The stun effect could be very useful in a fight, but unfortunately, he didn't own a shield at this time. Still, as Daniel thinks about the various sparring sessions he's had with Mary, Daniel can only choose Double Strike. It was only with a flurry of blows did he ever make her move, make her take him semi-seriously. Satisfied, he selects the Skill Proficiency and stares at his newly updated Status Screen.

Name: Daniel Chai
Class: Level 2 Adventurer (0%)
Sub-classes: Level 7 (Miner) (19%)
Human (Male)

Statistics
Life: 176
Stamina: 176
Mana: 136
Critical Hit Chance: 4%

Attributes
Strength: 17
Agility: 14
Constitution: 24
Intelligence: 15
Willpower: 17
Luck: 13

Skills
Unarmed Combat: Level 2 (47/100)
Clubs: Level 7 (21/100)
Shield: Level 5 (18/100)
Dodge: Level 3 (16/100)
Combat Sense: Level 2 (12/100)
Perception: Level 3 (21/100)
Mining: Level 7 (78/100)
Healing: Level 7 (07/100)
Herb Lore: Level 3 (31/100)
Cooking: Level 2 (37/100)
Singing: Level 2 (14/100)

Skill Proficiencies
Double Strike
Mapping (II)

Spells
Minor Healing (I)

Gifts
Martyr's Touch - The caster may heal oneself or others by touch and concentration, sacrificing a portion of his life to do so. Cost varies depending on the extent of the injuries healed.

Chapter 7

"Listen up, children." The guard in front of the dungeon entrance stares at the group of Adventurers before him. The beginner Adventurers grouped around him vary in size and clothing though most are in their mid-to-early teens and sport a single weapon, most often a short sword. The Adventurers are mostly human, though on occasion Daniel spots a Beastkin and even one dwarf in the group. "This is your first time in, so I strongly recommend you stick to the first floor. If you do manage to find the stairway to the second floor, you may go down but only to access the transportation gem. That'll allow you to travel to the second floor directly when you are ready to take it on.

"The number one cause of Adventurer deaths is overconfidence so don't think about going down to the second floor until you cleared the entire first floor. Never start a new floor injured - it's the fastest way to get yourself killed. Remember, the Guild buys mana stones of all sizes so make sure to collect every single drop that you get. The blacksmiths have asked me to remind all of you not to bring Kobold shanks back. They don't want them or need them. Any questions?"

Barely waiting for the Adventurers' answers, the guard steps aside and waves them into the Dungeon. Gripping his mace in hand, Daniel nods his thanks one last time before stepping in, his hand slightly clammy on the grip of his mace.

On entering, Daniel is immediately greeted by a simple stone room lit by the sunlight behind and the soft white glow characteristic of the Dungeon's mana-imbued walls.

Grinning slightly, Daniel shifts his bag once more to ensure it is properly seated before following the sole corridor that leads into the dungeon proper. The exit immediately splits into three earthen passageways, and Daniel pauses, listening for the movements of the other Adventurers before choosing the middle pathway.

As he moves deeper, a mental mini-map of the dungeon begins to form in his mind from the Mapping proficiency. Daniel gained that option as a Miner, like most others, and chose to level it up a couple of times rather than other more traditional mining proficiencies as he knew it'd be more useful for him in the future. You never wanted to be lost in the dark. *I wonder what other Adventurers do…*

Spending time thinking about inconsequential things like that is never a good idea in a Dungeon, a fact that Daniel finds out to his chagrin when he turns a corner and walks into a Kobold. A runt even among its kind, the three-foot-tall creature looks like a gray, gangly, slightly malnourished child clad in peasant garb, other than its rather elongated ears and too-wide eyes. Somehow, even after Mary's description, the Kobold looks nothing like he had pictured it. The Kobold reacts first, thrusting its only weapon, a shank made of metal and bone, into Daniel's chest. It hits hard, plunging through cloth and skin and grating against a rib. Daniel jumps backwards, groaning in pain as he feels blood begin to dribble from the wound, waving his mace to ward off the Kobold.

Taking to the offense, Daniel lashes out once and then again, the Kobold scurrying backwards and staying out of range of his attacks. As Daniel is recovering from his swings, the Kobold darts in again and attempts another stab, and only a last-minute hasty parry by Daniel forces the Kobold to stop its own attack or have its arm crushed.

Daniel again steps forwards, attempting to strike the Kobold who dances back and swings at Daniel's arm, nicking him. This fight is completely different from his earlier sparring matches with Mary. The Kobold is smaller, more prone to feints and is focused on short quick strikes to Daniel rather than a single painful attack.

As blood continues to run from his open wound, Daniel pushes forward to finish the fight. He throws another overhand right and then as the Kobold ducks, he charges forwards and activates Double Strike, his mace swinging faster as the proficiency activates. The first attack from the left is blocked, but using the force of the block, Daniel swings the mace around to strike on the Kobold's unprotected right side. The mace crunches into the Kobold's shoulder, cracking bone and mashing muscle.

Panicking, the Kobold pulls itself away from Daniel and attempts to stab its attacker again with its shank. This time, Daniel is ready though, and he smashes his mace onto the Kobold's outstretched attacking hand, crushing its fingers and forcing the monster to drop its weapon. As the Kobold flails, Daniel swings again, landing a Critical Strike on the top of the Kobold's head to deliver a fatal blow. A moment later, the body dissolves into acrid smoke leaving behind a small mana crystal.

Daniel barely pays attention, slumping into the corner and holding a hand over his wound as he chain casts Minor Healing on himself. It's only when the bleeding stops that he pays attention to the notifications he received during the battle.

Critical Hit! 29 Damage Dealt. Kobold killed.
Minor Healing cast on Daniel. 14 Hit Points Restored.
Minor Healing cast on Daniel. 10 Hit Points Restored.
Bleeding has stopped.

Seeing nothing important in the information, Daniel dismisses it and resolves to stop looking at such information. Daniel bends to pick up the dropped mana crystal, looking around warily before heading deeper into the dungeon. He'd used over nearly a third of his mana already, and he had just started. For the first time, he begins to truly understand Mary's point.

A half-dozen Kobolds later, and a chance meeting with one other Adventurer, and Daniel has found the staircase down. The other battles since the first one have gone quite well, with little additional damage dealt to him they have bolstered his flagging confidence. As long as he pays attention, with his skill and level, he should be able to deal with a single Kobold. Unlike most newbie Adventurers, this wasn't his first class, and as such, his Health was significantly higher than theirs. Of course, he had paid a price in time – most Adventurers who survived to his age were at a much higher level than him and would not even consider stepping into a Beginner Dungeon. Confident and impatient, Daniel makes a decision and takes the steps down, ignoring the guard's advice.

Chapter 8

The staircase down to the second floor leads to a small ten-foot-wide oval cavern that is currently empty. Unlike the first floor, the soft drip of water can be heard through the Dungeon; stalagmites and stalactites dot the floor and ceiling. Lighting on the second floor is worse too with the mana-imbued walls occasionally pitch black.

Daniel feels the hair on his arms stand out a little more; the second floor actually felt dangerous compared to the first. The exits from this cavern are smaller too, more cramped and Daniel soon realises he'll have to shorten some of his strikes. For a moment, he considers going back upstairs before he spots the portal stone and recalls the directions given. He walks over swiftly and places his hand on the stone where it gently lights up, 'remembering' his mana. The temporary distraction is enough to push the creeping doubts away.

"Let's see what I can find down here…" whispers Daniel to himself, filling the oppressive silence. It only takes a few minutes of walking for Daniel to run into his first Kobold, a far cry from the relatively quiet first floor. The fight does not take much more time than his fights on the first floor, though the Kobold is more skilled and is able to leave a long cut across his left arm. Daniel ignores the damage, only spending enough time to wrap a simple cloth bandage around his arm to stem the blood flow.

Emboldened by the successful fight, he journeys deeper into the dungeon, stopping only occasionally to check his surroundings and his mini-map to ascertain his location. Another fight with a Kobold brings him a third of the way to his next level up as an Adventurer. Obviously, actual Adventuring and fighting were a faster form of levelling than training.

It has been hours since the day began and the intense concentration required is wearing on him. The mental fatigue he is experiencing is something different from mining, and once again, his wandering mind betrays him as he doesn't notice the Kobold that creeps up behind him. His first impression of it is a sharp one, the shiv plunging into his back and nicking a kidney.

A hasty back kick glances off the Kobold's body, Daniel's larger size managing to push the monster away long enough for him to spin around. Daniel snarls, stepping forward and swinging his mace to injure the Kobold who ducks into the smaller passageway that it came from to dodge the strike. The side passage is much smaller, barely five feet in height with almost no lighting.

Daniel crouches to follow the shorter Kobold in, hoping to extract his revenge. Forced to shorten his swings and to jab the mace forwards in strikes, he doesn't have much room to attack properly, but the Kobold is still forced to back away from the stronger human or risk getting injured. Both parties trade insignificant blows for a few seconds, before another sharp pain in his buttocks makes Daniel realise that he's surrounded.

Trapped! For a moment, Daniel panics as the tight quarters, monsters in front and behind him and open wounds make his chest tighten and his vision narrow. He freezes, body locked in fear as he realises he might truly die here, his momentary pause allowing the Kobold he faces to lunge forward and stab his arm.

Instinctively, Daniel grabs the smaller Kobold's arm and holds the monster to him, picking the creature up and rushing forward to escape the confines of the passageway. Almost trampling the monster as he shoves the creature ahead of him, his panicked body attempts to create space away from his pursuing attacker and fails, the shiv from his attacker behind him plunging again into his back and eliciting another grunt of pain.

The Kobold he holds tight scratches and bites at the arm holding it but is unable to do significant damage without the use of its weapon. Daniel continues rushing ahead, crouched over and finally, the pathway breaks open into a larger room. Still gripping the Kobold, Daniel spins around and flings the smaller monster into its brethren's path before he falls back away from the two monsters, blood from his back continuing to pour out with every exertion.

In the larger room, Daniel's moment of panic begins to subside. The two monsters pull themselves apart and beginning to flank the novice Adventurer. Realising he cannot let them set themselves for an attack, Daniel rushes forward and activates his Double Strike proficiency, attacking the closest Kobold of the two. A pair of strikes lash out, one dodged but the second landing properly. It forces his attackers to grow warier as Daniel begins to swing his weapon with abandon, able to properly wind up in the larger space. Every time he is able to, he activates his skill proficiency, the mace suddenly moving faster.

It takes only a few more passes before the fight finishes, a lucky blow to the top of one attacker's skull stunning it long enough for a second attack to finish it. Faced one-on-one by Daniel, the second attacker falls with relative ease, and the injured Daniel slumps to the ground in pain. Out of battle, he feels the additional wounds on his arm and torso he received during the last few moments of desperate fighting.

Grunting in pain, Daniel focuses on calling forth his Gift and begins to stitch the wounds in his body together, cutting off the bleeding immediately. Once that important task is done, he proceeds to heal up the last of the damage with his mana, casting Minor Heal on himself and watching the last of the wounds stitch close.

"Well, that didn't go well…" Daniel whispers to himself before finally pulling himself to his feet. He looks around before sliding one of the Kobold shanks into his belt, finally recalling Mary's initial advice on having a shorter reach weapon on-hand. It definitely would have been helpful in the smaller passageway he had been trapped in. Thank Erlis he had more vitality and experience than a typical novice Adventurer. With a last stretch and quick looting of the mana stones, Daniel stares at his mini-map and ponders if he should head back upstairs or continue searching the second floor.

Chapter 9

"Damn. That's six." Sighing, the guard hands his friend a silver piece and shoots Daniel's tired form an unfriendly glare at his loss. Who would have thought that another beginner would show up this late at night? Most of the beginners from this morning's batch had called it a day hours ago, those that survived that is.

Daniel barely notices the look or the words, dragging his feet towards the awaiting Adventurer's Guild. He had long ago eaten all the food and drunk most of the water he had carried down, and he just wanted this to be over. Adventuring seemed to take more energy out of him than even the mines, and he was thoroughly ravenous. Vowing to carry more provisions the next time, all Daniel wants to do is to sell the mana stones he has collected and sleep.

In the Guild, Liev is finally coming to the end of his long shift when he spots Daniel. A flicker of relief breaks his professional facade as Mary would have been thoroughly upset if Daniel had died. His demeanor restored, he calls out, "Working hard I see!"

"Hi, Liev. Got a few stones for you…" Daniel empties the pouch on the counter, the shower of mana stones making Liev raise an eyebrow.

"That's quite a haul you have there…" Practised hands dance across the stones, pushing and sorting the stones by quality as he continues. "You went to the second floor didn't you?"

"Umm…"

"There are no rules barring that, Daniel. The Guild does not monitor, condone or judge such decisions. No matter how foolhardy," Liev states as he works on a piece of paper, totaling up Daniel's earnings.

"How did you know?"

"These here are all D Grade 12 stones and 11 stones, what I'd expect to see from the first floor. These three though are D Grade 10's which you'd only get if you were really lucky or were hunting on the second floor." As Liev speaks, he points to each pile before he twists his pad around and shows Daniel his total. Knowing that some of their clientele are unable to read, he states as well. "4 Silver and 3 Coppers. Third best haul among your group."

Daniel nods jerkily at the announcement automatically, picking up the coins as Liev deposits them on the counter. A decent amount, though an experienced miner could earn five silver a day for much less risk. After a moment, Daniel recalls what the attendant said, "Third?"

"Yes. Two of the Novices managed to find the chest on the first floor."

"Chest?" Feeling like a parrot, Daniel leans forward. Truth be told, after his nasty encounter on the second floor, he had grown a lot more careful and worked the second floor with caution, checking each side passageway carefully before moving on. Unfortunately, that meant he encountered Kobolds at a slower rate.

"You didn't even look for it did you?" Liev smiles, slightly bemused, reaching under his desk to pull out a mana stone. Almost the same size as the shards that Daniel has been bringing in, this one is noticeably clearer than his. "On each floor, there is a chest which contains a mana stone which is a number of grades higher than what you'd find defeating the mobs on that level. It moves around after it is found, respawning every two to four hours but it's always guarded by an Elite of that floor. This one here is a D Grade 8."

"Oh…" Daniel falls silent, tapping his fingers on the counter before looking up at Liev. "It's a matter of quantity over quality then isn't it? If I stay on the first floor, I'll be trying to find the chest to get a good, high-quality stone. If I go push down to the second floor again, I'll be able to fight more often, but it's more dangerous, and I wouldn't be able to get a chest yet."

Liev nods, internally surprised that Daniel has come to that conclusion that quickly. Most Adventurers take a while longer to work out those options by themselves.

"Thank you, Liev. I'll keep it in mind. Goodnight!" Daniel waves goodbye, moving away from the counter. It's been a long day, and it's time to get to bed.

***

"Morning, Daniel. Sleep in, did you?" A laughing Elise waves him over to the bar where she is busy cleaning up from the breakfast rush. "Breakfast will be out soon."

Daniel nods, plopping down onto the stool. He has his gear with him already, but a good meal to start the day seems like a great idea. That and coffee.

"So, Daniel. I know you saved my son and all…" Elise smiles as she drops a plate before him along with a steaming cup of coffee. "But you know, I run an Inn…"

Daniel blinks and then understands where Elise is leading with this and hangs his head slightly in shame, "Yeah, uhh… about that. How much for room and board for the week?"

"Since you're almost like family, a silver a day for all the food you can eat and we'll even wash your clothes," Elise pronounces unashamedly.

"Ummm… here you go." Daniel empties out the silver from his pouch, feeling how empty it is now. He shovels the last of the gruel in, already thinking of the Dungeon and refilling his purse and his many expenses. He will need a new shirt soon if he continues being stabbed so often, a shield to protect himself, soap to wash his clothing, another purse so that he can separate his mana stones from his coins. The list goes on.

As he finishes, Elise waves him towards a wrapped box that she has placed on the bar. "Here you go. Lunch and a snack."

"Thank, Elise. I'll be back late, I think." Scooping up the box, he stuffs it into his bag and hurries towards the Dungeon. He definitely needs to do better than yesterday, his current and future expenses piling up behind his eyes.

Watching his departing back, Elise smirks to herself. They were all like that, getting lazy after their first run. A little kick in their ass was what they needed. Whistling to herself, Elise walks back to the kitchen to begin washing up. That boy would do well.

Chapter 10

Waving to the guards as he passes them by, Daniel trots into the Dungeon's first floor without slowing down. A single Kobold didn't really pose too much danger to him after his experiences yesterday, certainly not those that lived on the first floor. However, unlike most other Adventurers, he had not bought a map, trusting his own proficiency to glean the layout. Recalling his talk with Liev yesterday, Daniel decides to work out the full layout of the first floor by himself and hopefully find the chest at the same time.

Moving at a slower pace once he is inside the actual dungeon, Daniel still paces through the passageways at a faster rate than the previous day, able to marvel at the strangeness of the dungeon. To his experienced eyes, the layout of the first floor made no logical sense as a cave network, even if it would to the ignorant. Small incongruities jumped out at Daniel; the floor was too smooth, the changes in the size of both the tunnels and chambers they joined making no natural sense and each cavern is too symmetrical. After encountering and killing a few more Kobolds, Daniel even begins to realise that the layout seems to repeat itself.

It takes Daniel almost three hours to make his way through three-quarters of the floor. He passes by a number of other novices, many moving more slowly and cautiously than he does. More than one pair have teamed up, an action that makes Daniel wonder before dismissing the option for now. At some point, he would need help, but a part of him revels at working alone after years of working in teams in the mine. In addition, he fears that any Adventurer he joined with would slow him down and he had a lot of ground to catch up on.

Not that I really want to deal with teenager angst either... Daniel chuckles to himself quietly, oblivious to the irony of his thoughts.

As he nears the next corner, Daniel hunches forward to peer into the chamber. His eyes widen, and he pulls his head back, hiding again. *Well, I found it. And him.*

Most Kobolds were four feet tall at most, but the Elite was obviously a paragon of its kind - standing four and a half feet tall and having actual, visible musculature. At least, what wasn't covered by what looked like badly-stitched-together soft leather armor. Thankfully, it was still armed with just a shiv.

For a moment, Daniel hesitates. Then, recalling that it was just a Kobold that at least two other beginners had beaten before him, he firms his resolve and steps out to meet the monster. The Kobold spots him almost immediately, growling a low challenge as it crouches down in front of the small chest.

Surprised that the Elite doesn't attack him straight away, Daniel hesitates before taking a step forward and throwing a cautious strike. The Kobold barely moves, seeing the feint for what it is.

Daniel's eyes widen further in surprise at this unexpected reaction, and he stops, hovering outside of the Kobold's reach. The Kobold moves first this time, throwing a rock it had concealed at Daniel. Instinctively, Daniel bats the rock aside and pays for it when his opponent lunges forward, plunging his weapon into Daniel's extended arm, twisting the blade as it exits to widen the wound. Before he can retaliate, the Kobold dances out of range again and flashes Daniel a predatory smile.

The next few passes have Daniel and the Kobold cautiously trading blows, neither fully committing to the attack. Daniel receives another light wound on his thigh, the Kobold suffering a bruised arm as it manages to foil a blow by pushing its arm forward into the mace's handle.

Frustrated, Daniel engages his double strike to watch the Kobold back away from the attacks, forcing Daniel to pursue him. A few more passes clarify Daniel's initial impressions. *Little bugger's fast. Hold still will you!*

Eyes narrow at a sudden thought and then Daniel shifts to slightly wider swings, focusing on herding the Kobold to a corner. It is his time to smile as the Kobold realises what is happening, but the human's greater reach foils the Elite's ability to get away even as Daniel receives a few more light injuries. Finally, backed into a corner, the Elite is unable to escape its end beneath the mace, though a last-minute surge by the monster leaves its shiv planted in Daniel's thigh as it dies.

Swearing to himself, Daniel collapses and tugs the shiv out of his thigh, slumping against the nearby wall as he takes his weight off his injured limb. A flash of red catches his eye at the passageway he entered, but he ignores it, focusing on healing himself first before turning to his notifications.

Level Up!
Adventurer Level 3
You have gained 5 attribute points to distribute.

Immediately, Daniel puts a few points into Agility before he shuts the window. He will figure out the rest tonight, but it is obvious to him that he needs to be faster against these monsters. Smiling in glee at the thought of the mana crystal that awaits him in the chest, he pushes himself up.

Was it open before? I was sure it wasn't... With dread filling him, Daniel walks over to the chest to find it empty with no sign of the thief.

***

"Bad day?" Liev asks the young Adventurer as he sorts and counts Daniel's mana stones. A slightly raised eyebrow at the lack of a more powerful mana stone, especially since the number that Daniel brought back was actually less than before. In fact, the way the stones told the story, Daniel must have spent most of his day on the first floor.

"I fought and defeated the Elite, but someone stole the stone while I was recovering," Daniel explains, looking morosely at the smaller number of coins Liev pushes forward as payment. Sighing, Daniel picks up the coins and puts them away.

"Ah, yes. That does happen occasionally." Liev shrugs, thievery in the Dungeon while uncommon was not unknown. Since there was no way to tell who owned a mana stone, thieves could steal stones with impunity in the Dungeon so long as they were not caught. Occasionally, bandits would even try their attempts at extortion or robbery, but those did not last long. Theft, while annoying, was an accepted part of Adventuring life. Since the only place to sell mana stones was at the Adventuring Guild, any bandit who came back with too great a haul regularly was bound to be caught.

Daniel nods glumly, having already decided not to make too much of a fuss over his loss. After all, he had no proof of who could have stolen his stone.

"Might I make a suggestion?" Liev smiles slightly at the young Adventurer, catching him just as he is about to leave.

"Of course." Daniel perks up, hoping for some earth-shattering advice from the experienced attendant. Surely he knew things that a young Adventurer could learn.

"There's a bathhouse a few blocks from the Top to the East. You'll find most Adventurers find it prudent to visit the bathhouses every few days." Liev smiles gently, eyeing the dirty, smelly Adventurer. Washcloth baths could only do so much, especially after a number of days fighting, killing and bleeding in the Dungeon.

"Oh!" Daniel blushes, realising Liev's unspoken implication. "Right. Thank you!" With that said, Daniel rushes off to the Top with what remains of his dignity.

Chapter 11

"15, 16, 17, 18!" Daniel sighs, staring forlornly at his small collection of coins as dawn light streams through the window. 1 Gold, 18 Silver. Still not enough to buy the shield he so desperately wanted. Armour, decent armour, was still a distant pipe dream, but a shield he could buy. Even with his increased skills and abilities, getting regularly wounded was becoming a pain.

A knock on his door brings Daniel out from his morose musings. "Yes?"

"Daniel, you're up?" Smiling Elise looks him over. "I need a little favour."

"What favour?" Daniel looks at innkeeper warily.

"Oh, nothing much. I just have a friend who needs some company today. You know, someone who needs to get out of work, stop doing the same things they've been doing non-stop," she smiles slightly while looking at him knowingly.

"Umm… well, I was going to go to the Dungeon…," Daniel mutters. He ignores the implication Elise makes, even though he has yet to take a break in the three weeks since he has first entered the Dungeon.

"It's fine; you'll love it. Anyway, you haven't really seen much of the town yet, have you? This would be a great opportunity, and it'd let you get in some shopping." She points to his rather threadbare, often-patched set of clothing.

A short twenty minutes later, Daniel is standing outside the Spinning Top, muttering about a wasted day and wondering who this friend was. When Khy'ra walks up, he can't help but smile at the blonde elf. He has barely had time to visit the Clinic with his activities, and when he has done so, it has often been late at night after returning from the Dungeon when Khy'ra was not around. "Khy'ra! It's good to see you."

"And you. Did you see Elise…?" Khy'ra is looking around, frowning. "She asked me to come over."

"Umm…."

"Good, you're both here." Stepping out of the inn as she wipes her hands on her apron, Elise nods firmly. "Kyra, Daniel needs a guide around town. He's yet to actually see anything, and he could do with some new clothes too."

"What…?"

"Oh and don't bother going to the Clinic or the Dungeon. I told them not to let you guys in." Smirking, Elise walks back briskly into the Top and shuts the door behind her.

"Couldn't she be a bit more subtle…" mutters Khy'ra as she stares at the door, blushing slightly.

"Yeah…" Daniel agrees with her before he tilts his head, struck by a thought. "Do you mean…?"

"Shopping!" Smiling brightly, Khy'ra grabs his hand and drags him down the street. "I know just the place for some new clothing."

"Actually… I was saving up for something."

"Something?" An arched eyebrow has Daniel quickly explaining.

"A shield. I'm getting stabbed a lot, especially when I'm fighting two Kobolds. It'd be nice to be able to guard one side properly. Nothing too big of course, it's a bit cramped you know, but yeah…" Daniel trails off, realising explaining the intricacies of using a shield to Khy'ra might be a bit much.

"Then let's go!" She tugs Daniel down the street, half-dragging the man down to the river with her. "So, you're a mace and shield fighter, eh? I'd have thought Mary would have converted you to the sword."

Daniel laughs, shaking his head. "She's amazing, but the sword requires real skill to use, you know? And the mace just feels right."

"Oh, I get that. I hated the sword myself. Especially in those tunnels! I could barely swing without hitting the walls at times." Khy'ra reminisces, miming a swinging action as she speaks.

"You were an Adventurer?" Daniel tilts his head to Khy'ra, bemused at the thought of the bubbly creature beside him in the depths of the dungeon, searching for Kobolds and killing them with a smile.

"Yes. I was one of the first to enter this Dungeon actually. Came here with my brothers." Khy'ra smiles, shaking her head reminiscing. "We couldn't get the reward for completing it first though, and they left soon after. I decided to stay for a bit. Here we are."

Daniel nods comfortably as she talks, both of them weaving through the busy morning traffic. It takes him a moment to realise that the last sentence wasn't part of the initial conversation and he looks up to spot the sign of an armourer swinging above him. Even as he gets pulled inside, Daniel realises where they are.

"Maxwell, I have a customer for you - we need your best shields," Khy'ra announces as they enter the armoury, the forge at the back increasing the temperature a few degrees even out at the front of the shop.

Stepping away from his forge and beckoning to an apprentice to take over, Maxwell grins as he spots Khy'ra, "Definitely not for you. Oh, it's you!" He nods firmly to Daniel while he gestures behind him to where the shields hang. "Stock hasn't changed."

Daniel smiles politely, stepping further into the shop to survey the pair of styles available. A simple buckler and a larger round wooden shield, both banded by metal are his choices. His fingers trace the round wooden shield with lust, the larger shield perfect for his fighting style and what he has been saving up for before he looks to Maxwell and asks, "A gold and fifty still?"

Maxwell nods before Khy'ra clears her throat loudly. "You know, Max, Daniel here has been helping out a lot at the Clinic lately. Why, he helped me deal with that rather nasty situation with Peony. And her friends."

"Peony?" Maxwell's face goes blank. "I don't, well, if he's been the one helping you, Khy'ra… A gold and…" A slight smile from Khy'ra makes him stop. "A gold."

Daniel watches the byplay, a small part of him feeling slightly guilty about the deal. It is only a small part though as he snatches up the shield and pushes the gold into Max's hand. "Thank you! A gold it is."

The pair spends the rest of the day shopping, stopping by to pick up some basic household supplies for both themselves and some additional supplies for the Clinic. Khy'ra occasionally name drops Daniel and his connection to the Clinic, though Daniel finds it hard to understand when and why she does so. After a time, he gives up on it and just enjoys her company, the two chatting amicably about Khy'ra's past exploits and the city.

While they shop, Khy'ra takes her role as guide seriously, pointing out reputable shops and food establishments as well as laying down town gossip with undisguised glee. Having lived in the city for over twenty years and being one of the original inhabitants, Khy'ra is a fount of information about local history, and more than once, Daniel is amazed by the knowledge that she exhibits. It is clear to Daniel that Khy'ra holds a deep affection for the town and its inhabitants, one that she is happy to impart to him.

Evening finds them on a hill overlooking the town at Khy'ra's bequest, a small indulgence that takes her away from the city. The first snows of the winter have yet to arrive so while the evening has a brisk air to it, they were still dry, and the chill kept the hill empty except for themselves. As the sun sets, Daniel takes a moment to truly look at the town he has spent so many weeks in.

Karlak is bisected a third of the way in its circumference by a river, surrounded by a lightly patrolled wooden wall. Built between the rolling forested hills that make up the vast majority of the lands around here, Karlak draws its stone and ore from the distant mountains that Daniel came from. Lying on the outer frontier of Brad's borders, the town is surrounded by unexplored forests, connected by a network of dusty roads. The vast majority of the buildings in the town are made up of the easily secured wood, clay tiles or dirty rushes marking differences in prosperity from the hilltop.

"You puzzle me, Daniel." Khy'ra, propped up on her elbow stares at the young man next to her, interrupting his thoughts. "Are you really that naive or just that nice?"

"Huh?" Daniel, caught off guard, blinks at the non-sequitur.

"You don't exploit your Gift. You don't even mention your connection to the Clinic to the merchants we visit. Yet you use it without hesitation…"

"Ah…" Daniel sighs, flopping over to stare up into the darkening sky. That question. Why always that question? He raises his hand up, shading himself from the non-existent sunlight for a moment before he speaks. "My grandfather, he used to say, do good, just don't ever expect gratitude. What I do, when I heal, it isn't for them."

"Then who is it for?"

"Me." Daniel shuts his eyes. He falls silent, letting the word stand between them. Unwilling and unable to explain the extent of guilt that he harbors, that comes from having a gift like his and not exploiting it to the fullest. The constant pressure by others the moment his Gift manifested, the constant demands to use it, to be someone important. The pressure and the fear of even more were why he didn't speak of the extent of his Gift, both its cost and its full ability. The less people knew, the less they could use against him. This way, they could ask, they could suspect, but they couldn't know.

Pursing her lips, Khy'ra watches the play of emotions on his face before making up her mind. She swings her leg over his prone body, straddling him to lay a kiss on his lips. As his eyes pop open, she smiles. "Well, Elise did set this up. So, are we?"

Laughing, Daniel rolls her over and returns the kiss, banishing deeper considerations for the moment.

Chapter 12

A shiv comes speeding towards his left eye, but Daniel doesn't flinch, raising the shield just enough to catch the light blade. Once his arm begins moving, he trusts instinct to get it in the way correctly and focuses instead on lashing out at his other attacker and triggering Double Strike. The first blow is hastily dodged by the Kobold, the second crushing its knee.

Rather than pushing his luck, Daniel jumps back to separate himself from his assailants. He catches the second Kobold's attack on his shield again and deflects it to the side this time, creating an opening for his mace to crash down onto the monster's head. The Kobold staggers under the blow, a choked scream emanating from it as it struggles to stand up but is quickly dispatched before Daniel focuses on the remaining maimed Kobold to finish the fight.

Exhaling in relief and concentrating to slow his breathing down, Daniel checks his surroundings quickly before pocketing the mana stones. Still no sign of that damn red cloak... Pushing the thought away, Daniel grins over the progress he has made. Another level and a shield have made the second floor and the Kobolds warriors he fights significantly easier to handle. A higher level of Agility means that he can now keep up with the Kobolds and their fast, short attacks, while his greater strength allows him to occasionally smash aside their defenses with impunity.

Looking at his mini-map and the two passageways that split before him, he picks the one on the right where a larger cavern awaits. He knows that the larger cavern will normally hold a few more Kobolds if it had not been cleared already by another Adventurer. Hunting Kobolds was almost fun now that he wasn't getting stabbed nearly every other fight.

Two hours of further fighting, and he finally gets the notification he's looking for.

Level Up!
Adventurer Level 4
You have gained 5 attribute points and 1 Skill Proficiency to distribute

He doesn't even have to think about it, having spent more than a few idle nights plotting what attributes and proficiencies he requires to progress further. A quick selection and he pulls up his Status page to review the results.

Name: Daniel Chai
Class: Level 4 Adventurer (1%)
Sub-classes: Level 7 (Miner) (19%)
Human (Male)

Statistics
Life: 201
Stamina: 201
Mana: 152

Attributes
Strength: 18
Agility: 19
Constitution: 26
Intelligence: 16
Willpower: 18
Luck: 13

Skills
Unarmed Combat: Level 3 (01/100)
Clubs: Level 9 (11/100)
Shield: Level 5 (78/100)
Dodge: Level 4 (36/100)
Combat Sense: Level 6 (72/100)
Perception: Level 5 (16/100)
Mining: Level 7 (78/100)
Healing: Level 7 (47/100)
Herb Lore: Level 3 (31/100)
Cooking: Level 2 (37/100)
Singing: Level 2 (14/100)

Skill Proficiencies
Double Strike
Shield Bash
Mapping (II)

Spells
Minor Healing (I)

Gifts

Martyr's Touch - The caster may heal oneself or others by touch and concentration, sacrificing a portion of his life to do so. Cost varies depending on the extent of the injuries healed.

Satisfied, Daniel continues his search for the chest. It is another hour before he locates it, the second floor significantly larger than the first and consequently requiring much more time to map and search. He's not even surprised to see two Elite Kobolds guarding the chest. The second floor's guardians seemed to vary depending on the luck of the Adventurer, either presenting a single Elite and a regular Kobold or two Elites.

Checking behind himself once more to ensure he is not followed by an opportunistic Kobold, or a red cloak, Daniel peeks about the corner till both of the Kobolds are no longer facing his entrance. He sprints forward immediately, keeping as silent as a 5' 8" man carrying a shield and mace can be in the cave. It gets him about halfway there before the first Kobold notices him, screaming a warning that is cut short soon after as Daniel gets close enough, at last, to swing with his mace down overhand to crush the creature. Only a last-minute jerk of its head saves the Elite Kobold's life, but the mace still smashes into its shoulder to crack the collarbone and drive it to its knees.

The moment his feet are set, Daniel spins and utilizes Shield Bash on the other Elite who is already winding up its own strike. Daniel's attack is hastily thrown, but it smashes into the out-thrust shiv with force, sending the shiv and arm spinning aside. The Elite is not stunned, but Daniel now has more than enough time and space to face his first opponent and engage Double Strike. A fast series of strikes, both hitting for once, manages to end the injured Elite's life.

Daniel doesn't pause, already turning to deal with his last opponent. His quick turn keeps the Elite's strike from doing more than superficial damage to his arm, and Daniel hunches down beneath his shield, ready to finish the fight. The remainder of the fight is relatively one-sided, though much less spectacular as Daniel hounds the Elite with quick, fast strikes that force the Kobold to defend itself till a failed attempt at a dodge ends it.

As is his tradition now, the moment the monster falls Daniel spins around to check his surroundings. Still no red cloak. He strides quickly to the chest to take his rightful prize before collecting the remaining mana stones, a wide smile on his face. Today was definitely a good day.

Chapter 13

"Har!" Daniel grins, feeling the shiv skid off his newly bought chausse. No more getting stabbed in the thigh by these too-short monsters. It was a pain trying to block attacks that came so low with his shield - he either had to stay crouched really low for hours on end or keep his shield at a comfortable height and risk missing a block. A few weeks later, Daniel finally has some armor after more skimping and saving. It cost him more than he cared to think about, nearly three times what he would have needed to live on as a miner, but it was worth every penny.

Of course, Daniel isn't wasting time just gloating. His mace whistles down in a diagonal strike onto the Kobold he has been targeting, smashing it into the ground. As the Kobold attempts to stand, he winds up and kicks it in the side, keeping his shield close to him to foul probing attacks from the other two Kobolds he faces. The kick picks up the smaller monster, smashing it into his friends and throwing the group off-balance.

A chained attack that keeps the group of Kobolds staggering and injured ending with a Double Strike ends the fight soon after. New armor, new tactics, and another level have boosted Daniel's fighting abilities significantly. He confidently fights two or three Kobolds these days without fail, only receiving the most minor of injuries in most cases. Daniel no longer even bothers with trips to the first or second floor, only working the third floor and the more numerous Kobolds there. Until today though he has avoided the location where the Sector boss and main floor boss lived, preferring to work his skills safely. Today though was the day he would challenge the monster.

The trip to the Kobold Chief's lair takes Daniel another hour, the Adventurer pausing after each battle to rest and recuperate. As he nears the chamber, he hears a scream, and he picks up his pace. His sudden, noisy entrance surprises the combatants for a second, giving Daniel time to assess the situation.

An Adventurer is curled up on the floor missing his arm, bleeding out while his companion stands facing the Kobold Chief. She is the screamer, her sword and dagger combo wavering as fear grips her. The Kobold Chief sports a single large gash on its arm but is otherwise unharmed. To Daniel's surprise, the Chief is no taller than a normal Kobold at a short four feet though the monster wields an actual short sword, chipped as it is and wears rusted chainmail for protection on its torso. The other major change in appearance is that the Kobold Chief is significantly more muscular than a regular Kobold with defined musculature in its arms and chest.

Pushing aside other thoughts, and concerns for the other Adventurers, Daniel rushes the Kobold Chief who jumps away with ease and speed. The movement is quicker than any of his previous opponents by a significant margin.

Narrowing his eyes over the shield, Daniel hunkers down for a long fight, realising that he cannot take chances here. Recalling his first fight with an Elite, Daniel begins to feint and attack with wider swings, intent on cornering the Chief.

The Chief growls at Daniel, deflecting a swing with the mace with its own short sword, but Daniel's surprising strength throws it aside slightly, forcing the Kobold to compensate for its balance by taking a step backwards. As it recovers, Daniel's backhand catches the Chief on its forehead, sending the creature stumbling again. Daniel steps forward again to push his advantage but is distracted by the sound of metal on stone behind him. The female Adventurer, exhausted and panicked, has dropped to her knees, her weapons clattering against the ground.

Daniel turns back to his fight, having taken his eyes away from the Kobold but for a second, and is greeted by black smoke rising from where the Kobold Chief was. A tentative swing through the smoke shows that it is just smoke, so Daniel spins around searching for his opponent.

The Chief reappears behind the shocked female Adventurer. Shouting a warning, Daniel is too late as the Chief stabs downwards, targeting not the female Adventurer but her injured friend, cutting his throat with relish. Screaming in anger, Daniel crosses the floor and Shield Bashes the bloodthirsty smile from the Kobold, watching the creature stumble back stunned. Not giving the creature any further chances, Daniel smashes it with quick strikes, his technique falling by the wayside as rage consumes him.

Daniel is panting and leaning over after the Chief finally falls, having never let the monster a respite after the original stun. Somewhere along the way, the Kobold Chief had managed to slip a thrust under his breastplate, right above his hips and only now does Daniel truly feel it. He has no time though to worry about his own wounds as he hurries over to the pair of Adventurers.

"Miss. Are you okay?" Provided no answer, he places a hand on her shoulder and sends his Gift into her body, finding nothing major to heal. He bends down to touch the armless corpse, again sending the energy of his Gift out in forlorn hope. It finds no purchase in the soulless corpse, coming back to him and Daniel bows his head in silent grief for the two for a moment.

Unable to do anything for either, he turns his attention back to his own injuries and the loot. A series of quick Heals puts him right again before he loots the room. Coming back to the body, he rolls the Adventurer over and does a quick search, pulling out the money pouch from the Adventurer's body. He presses the pouch into the lady's hand and helps her sheath her weapons. The Adventurer responds to direct instructions and guiding hands but otherwise does little else, her body already beginning to shiver from shock.

Hours later, Daniel finally manages to guide the lady out of the Dungeon. The moment the setting sun hits her face, she screams and rips off her belt and weapon, throwing them onto the ground before running away from the Dungeon. Daniel steps toward her fleeing form but is stopped by a hand on his shoulder.

"Don't." Daniel turns to see the guard, the one who lost the bet on his first night out. Brown concerned eyes stare out from a bearded face as he holds the young Adventurer still. "We'll keep an eye on her, make sure she doesn't do any harm. To herself or others. Then when it's time, we'll get her to a Priest. You did your part; you got her out."

Daniel slowly nods. A part of him wants to help, but mostly, he's glad. His Gift was powerful, but it had limits, and the mind was one thing he could not heal. This was outside his purview, "Okay."

On the other side, the guard's larger, balding companion bends down to pick up the weapon sheath, belt and its attached coin purse for safekeeping. The bearded guard considers Daniel, tilting his head in thought, "You don't look too shaken. Most newbies find their first death hard to deal with."

Daniel grunts, looking back into the Dungeon before he answers, "It's not my first. The mines weren't safe either."

The guard grins, clapping Daniel on the shoulder. "Good man. Keep that in mind and you might just make it to the bottom. The name's Ken, and that silent lunk is Curtzman."

"Daniel." Daniel looks back to the entrance before he mutters about what is bothering him, "I left his body back there. Couldn't carry it and watch her…"

"Don't bother; it's gone. The Dungeon will have taken it already. That's the Adventurer's Grave for you." Ken shrugs before he shoves Daniel on the shoulder. "Best hand in your stones; you're buying tonight at the Top."

Daniel opens his mouth to protest the guard's insistence, but after a moment, shuts it. He did need a drink, and rough and selfish as it was, the invitation was meant in a friendly manner. "Tonight then."

Chapter 14

A finger traces down his chest as Khy'ra smiles at Daniel in her bed. Outside, the town was blanketed in white from another snowfall, broken up by the criss-crossing tracks of carts getting ready for the day's work. The last few weeks had deepened the budding relationship between the elf and human, though due to their nature and profession, an agreed upon mutual emotional distance was still kept. Life had fallen into a comfortable routine, seeing each other when their schedules allowed, but neither insisting on more than the other would give.

For Khy'ra, the relationship with Daniel would always be a temporary one, as any relationship with one not as long-lived. It was a curse of their kind and why so few Elves deigned to live and work amongst the shorter-lived races. Few desired to deal with the emotional toll of watching one after another of their friends grow close and die, again and again. Khy'ra herself was considered highly unusual, not only on her insistence in interacting with the shorter-lived races but by becoming a healer amongst them. It would not be entirely fair to say that other elves saw her work among the destitute humans and Beastkin as futile, a delaying of the inevitable, but it was not far off.

"How are things going?" Khy'ra asks, just enjoying touching Daniel's hairless chest. Certainly, she might be slightly unusual, but she felt no carnal desire for those hairy rugs that many other humans and dwarves sported.

"Mmm… good. Very good. I went down to the fourth floor yesterday, registered myself, and then finished the third again. I think, I think I'm ready to try tomorrow." He rolls over, kissing her and grins as he waggles his eyebrows. "Today's another… shopping… day though."

She snorts, pushing at Daniel's chest. "No…. some of us actually have to work."

Grinning, Daniel plays his trump card, leaning down and gently nibbling on her pointed ears. She moans slightly, whispering softly, "Maybe I can be late…"

***

Whistling as he leaves Khy'ra's house, Daniel reflects on his luck these past few months. The initial free training gave him a leg-up, honing his fighting skills sufficiently to let him utilise more advanced attacks and tactics than see-smash. In the last few weeks, at first reluctantly but now routinely, he has joined Ken, Curtzman and the other guards and even some senior Adventurers drinking at the Top in the evening when he comes back. Elise kept an eye on the young Adventurer when he did so, often cutting him off and sending him to rest when he stayed too long, her mothering done with the deft hand of an experienced innkeeper.

It was the advice from the Adventurers and guards that drove his agenda for this shopping trip. The fourth floor saw a major change in the dungeon layout with the introduction of the Draxillan Crawler and Dungeon-built traps. The Draxillian Crawler was a strange beast that was tougher individually than any Kobold, skittering around in its grey shell and twelve legs up walls and down passageways with ease. The monsters routinely avoided traps that caught unwary Adventurers. However, their greatest threat was not in their fighting prowess but what they defecated. Joined together, the Crawlers feces and a chemical it extruded were mixed together to create a fast hardening substance that had the strength of stone. It was highly prized among the construction companies, but in the Dungeon, the Crawlers would often cover chamber entrances and exits, constantly changing the layout of the floor and driving Adventurers into traps and cul-de-sacs.

The city hired Adventurers to constantly break down the newly-created blockages, but it was a constant battle that made the Guild-sold map of the floor both a necessity and a waste.

"4 vials of glow moth serum, 40 feet of rope, attachment for the ropes and a hammer." In the general store, Daniel lists his requirements to the proprietor. "Also, 2 dozen trap balls, a dozen bushels of sage and the cotton balls."

The proprietor of the store, a short older man, hurries off before coming back with the goods neatly packed. "Fourth floor?"

Daniel nods as he pays before he is stopped by the proprietor whose hand comes back from under the counter with a smaller glass canister with glow crystals shedding a soft, warm light. "For you. It can get dark down there. Good luck, Daniel."

Daniel automatically takes the light, at the same time querying, "Have we met?"

"Not me. My cousin works at the Clinic and pointed you out a while ago."

"Oh…" Daniel nods his thanks, taking the bundle and heading to the armourer. Like most Adventurers, Daniel's interactions with the regular townsfolk was limited to a select few shops that directly catered to their needs. Armourers, blacksmiths, the apothecary, a few inns where the Adventurers congregated. Yet a town could not survive just on those things, and outside of the Adventurers' direct sphere of interactions lay farmers, tailors, shopkeepers, masons and more who thrived off the funds that flowed from the Dungeon. It was only Daniel's continued presence at the Clinic, and his relationship with Khy'ra, that highlighted his presence to the townsfolk.

At the armoury, Max pokes at Daniel's pauldrons before making him jump in place while holding his hands up to ensure it fitted properly. Grunting in acceptance, Max makes Daniel spin around again and bend over, checking the links and closures before Max finally grunts acceptance at the work, "It'll do."

"Thanks, Max. It feels great, just great. I barely even feel the weight anymore," Daniel gushes, grateful for the free fitting that Max offered to do last night. He even cleaned some of the blood off the used armor, bringing it back at least partly to its glory days before Daniel's abuse.

"The fourth floor is bad enough without adding ill-fitting armour. You just come back for some proper steel armour before you reach the seventh, yes? Those Ogres will smash right through this," Max says.

Nodding enthusiastically, Daniel makes his final payment and heads out, not even bothering to get undressed. The newly refitted armor was so comfortable, and Daniel secretly thought he looked rather dashing in it. He couldn't wait to try the fourth floor tomorrow.

***

"I hate the fourth floor," grouses Daniel as he slumps in his seat next to his usual drinking partners the next evening. Draining his mug, he waves to Elise for a refill.

"Har!" A huge hand claps his back, sending Daniel sprawling forward in his seat as Ken and his friends laugh at the new Adventurer. "Now, you're a real Adventurer."

"Real Adventurer?" Daniel says.

"Oh yeah, you ain't one till you've done the fourth floor." Laughing, Ken raises his glass and voice, "To the Crawlers!"

The cheers and resounding toasts make Daniel look around suspiciously. Ken smiles and explains, "There are two groups of adventurers who go to the fourth floor. We call them the farmers and the Adventurers. Farmers love it - it's good, consistent money killing the Crawlers for their stones and sacs. Combine it with being paid by the Guild to open up the passageways, and you can earn a decent living. That's them…" Ken nods to those who joined his toast.

"Then there's the real Adventurers. You guys hate the middle floors because all you want to do is get strong and get down. Not easy to do when you spend half the day checking for traps, backtracking from dead-ends that weren't there the day or even hour before and only occasionally fighting.

"You, kid, you're an Adventurer. Knew it the first time we talked."

Daniel sighs and nods his head in acceptance. The fourth floor, with proper preparation, wasn't hard. It was just slow and frustrating.

"Just remember, kid, it's all good training. Don't rush it - the Ogres in the next sector would squash you flat," says Ken.

***

Ken's cautious advice still ringing in his mind, Daniel is up and early again the next morning. If it were not for the fact that Crawlers had significantly better mana crystals than the Kobolds, he would have seen an even more drastic drop in his income, even with the addition of the sale of the chemical sacs which were an additional part of the loot. As it stood, he still had lost a third of his regular income yesterday.

Journeying to the fourth floor via portal stone, Daniel readies himself before touching the stone. He gasps as the mana from the stone flows out and enters his body, the cold so intense that he is unable to breathe for a moment before pins and needles shoot through his body. The pain is exquisite and lasts for a moment before he finds himself on the fourth floor next to the portal stone. Daniel raises his shield automatically, crouching down and finds no enemy waiting for him, only then relaxing and stopping his shivers.

Mentally surveying the map he created yesterday, Daniel picks the path to the right, climbing over fallen rocks to peer into the cramped passageway. He moves forward cautiously, pushing against the stone with his mace at each step, ensuring that it is solid and able to take his weight before he moves forward.

The passageway is short, breaking out into a small cavern. He pulls a trap ball from his pocket, dropping it beneath him to test the ground before eyeing the corners of the cavern. Seeing no additional problems, he clambers down from the passageway slowly and picks up the ball to send it rolling across the floor ahead of him.

In this way, Daniel journeys through another two passageways before he encounters his first Crawler of the day. The Crawler is squatted at the end of the passageway that Daniel is walking through, patting newly laid waste into shape as it secretes the chemical from its mouth. Daniel spots the creature first and takes off at a run, hoping to catch it unaware. That hope is dashed as the Crawler looks up at the last second, swinging its carapace clad body to the side and shedding part of Daniel's blow. Skittering legs on one side start moving as it backs away, intent on giving itself space to attack Daniel, but it is hampered by the Adventurer smashing some of those legs into paste.

In pain, the Crawler swings its body back to Daniel and attempts to use its greater weight to crush the smaller Adventurer. Daniel jumps back, barely able to dodge the monster in the cramped confines of the cavern they fight in. He swings again, crushing a mandible as the monster rears back to bite him and then as it reacts to the pain, he smashes his mace upwards before triggering a Shield Bash. The Crawler staggers backwards, injured, and Daniel pushes his advantage. Too fast, for he forgets that the creature can swing its back too. The blow catches Daniel high up on his body and smashes him into a nearby wall.

Daniel struggles back to his feet, shoulder and chest in pain, but the Crawler is hurt too. Shouting in anger, Daniel stands and jumps forward, bringing his hammer down onto the creature's head, braining it and ending the fight. Panting, Daniel waits for the smoke to dissipate before collecting both sac and mana.

A good start, though painful. Now to find more monsters, he thinks as he walks off into the passageway. Slow and patient, that was the way to go.

Chapter 15

"No."

Daniel jerks to a stop, pulling his foot back from the step he was about to take. He turns to survey the area, only then spotting the figure seated on an out-cropping a few feet to his right. He frowns, the figure, covered in an extremely dirty cloak, is tiny but looks utterly relaxed.

It is his first day on the fifth floor, and so far, it has been every bit as frustrating as the fourth floor, if not more so. Traps, delays, surprise attacks and more. He hunches down, trying to spot the problem while he speaks, "Why?"

"Trap."

"I figured." Daniel huffs and then takes hold of his irritation. "Thank you. But what kind of trap is it?"

"Deadfall." Seeing Daniel's puzzled face, she points up.

He looks up and eyes the stalactite before slowly taking a deep step back. A single ball has already rolled over the ground, part of the precautions he uses, so he pulls two now and rolls both at the same time down the corridor. This time, the pressure is sufficient to cause the trap to trigger and one other trap further down the corridor.

"Noisy." Its hands raised to its head, the other Adventurer hops down lightly next to Daniel. The figure before him surprises Daniel for a brief moment; Beastkin were an uncommon sight, though he knew that they made up a higher proportion of the Adventuring population than their minority numbers would lead one to believe. Standing just slightly shorter than his own 5' 8", he notes it is a feline Beastkin with black fur and wide, jade eyes. She leans forwards, her whiskers tickling his face from her slightly elongated muzzle as she sniffs him before dropping down from her tiptoes, her proximity giving him a quick whiff of her fragrant musk. A part of him notes that she looks more animalistic than many others, more like a grown Jaguar forced to walk upright than a human with Cat features. From his time in the city, he knew that the Beastkin varied greatly in their appearance, though many leant towards more human in appearance. The female Adventurer points down the way, indicating the leftmost branch as she continues to speak. "Hive. Help?"

He puzzles over her words for a few moments before he realises she's asking him to join up to deal with the hive. Daniel has only run across a small hive once before, and the fight had left him drained and injured. A half-dozen Crawlers, even with his new armor had nearly been his undoing. "Maybe. How many?"

"One. Two. Many?" She pauses, watching him wince before grinning at her own joke. "Nine."

He snorts, brown eyes tightening in thought as he runs the odds in his head. "Yeah, okay."

She grins widely at him, stepping forward and leading the way. When he gets to the balls, Daniel picks them both up, noting one is badly chipped.

He sighs, realising he might need to go shopping again soon as his stock is nearly depleted.

It only takes ten minutes for them to make their way to the hive. Peering in, Daniel grimaces and looks at his new companion to speak about strategies. Daniel is too late though, and he just catches the quick movements of the Catkin as she ducks past him, already throwing knives at the Crawlers.

Daniel groans, rushing forward to attack the nearest monster, noting it's been blinded already by the Beastkin's accurate throws. He smashes his club down, crushing the carapace before booting the monster up and then smashing it aside with his shield onto another incoming monster.

The first monster slain, Daniel steps back, resetting his stance as he readies himself to fight the swarm of crawlers that have targeted him. At the corner of his eye, he notes the Catkin has swarmed up the side of the cavern and is throwing her knives to distract and injure the foes that rush him now, ignoring the pair that have begun crawling up the wall to her. The blades are well aimed, most finding gaps in the carapace, but after even a few moments of fighting, Daniel judges that the throwing knives are no more than painful annoyances for these creatures. It will be up to him to finish their opponents off.

Sliding to the right, he dodges a lunge by a Crawler and activates Double Strike, smashing its legs on one side before he boots the creature away again. Another attack is caught on his shield, and he takes the time to Shield Bash this assailant, using its temporary disorientation to land a few more blows. Even as he finishes dealing with that monster, another one takes his first opponents place, mandibles skittering off his armour as it fails to gain purchase.

The battle is hard pressed, the Crawlers swarming Daniel at every turn. Forced to focus on damaging and hampering them, Daniel is unable to finish a kill as he continually moves and attacks. A bad step though has him lose balance for a precious moment, one that a Crawler uses to attach itself to his leg and yank him off his feet. Its mandibles close on his shin attempting to shatter the bone, delayed only for a brief period by his greaves.

The Catkin's jump onto the creature from her perch smashes it down, and she reaches forward, daggers plunging into the Crawler's eyes. It releases Daniel who scrambles back and onto his feet as the Catkin jumps away, neatly avoiding an attack from behind.

The remainder of the fight passes without further life-threatening incidents and, in the end, Daniel slumps amongst the bodies, sweat covering him and sticking his brown hair to his face. He pulls his helmet off to let it cool, noting that the Catkin does not seem to be sweating at all. Then again, did cats sweat? After a brief rest, they work to collect the mana stones and the additional sac drops. Thankfully, they didn't need to haul the faeces upstairs - the hired Adventurers who worked for the Guild did that with the broken-down exits where alchemists dissolved them again into their component parts to await the chemical sacs.

Housekeeping done, Daniel turns to the Catkin who is busy cleaning her daggers with a cloth and water. "Thank you."

"More?" She points down the way while putting away her cloth amongst an impressive array of knives.

"Why not?"

***

"Why haven't I partied up before?" Daniel muses to himself as they exit the Dungeon after a very successful day into a brisk winter weather. The Catkin's ability to sense traps and sniff out the Crawlers meant that he travelled faster and backtracked less today. On the other hand, more than once, he was able to help guide her around a faster entrance or exit due to his own mapping skill. And it was obvious, at least to Daniel, that the Catkin had been having trouble fighting the Crawlers. She could kill one or two on her own without issue, but on the fifth floor, the Crawlers often came in larger numbers. Without the raw strength to shatter their carapace, the Catkin must have been forced to fight a battle of slow attrition in great danger to herself.

There was one thing that bothered Daniel about their partnership though, and as the Catkin heads off, he rushes forward to touch her on the shoulder. She snarls, hunching down and popping a pair of claws before realising it's him and relaxing slightly, though she still backs away from the Adventurer.

"Sorry! I just don't know your name." Daniel apologises, pulling his hand back.

"Asin," she purrs resting a hand on her chest. She points to him and mutters, "Daniel."

"Yeah." He wonders how she knows his name, but dismisses it. "You know, we did pretty well. Do you want to do this again tomorrow?"

Asin pauses, looking the young man up and down. Daniel was not unknown to her, the Clinic was one of the few locations that took in Beastkin for treatment, and as such, all the workers in the Clinic had a level of notoriety among the Beastkin minority in Karlak. In addition, she has secretly watched the young man's progress for the last few days as he worked through the level. In truth, Daniel's judgements about her progress were spot on, and she had been considering travelling back up a floor to gain strength before attempting the fifth floor. All these thoughts pass through her head quickly before she nods affirmatively, waving goodbye to the young man as she heads into the Guild to sell their collected loot.

***

"I tell you, my cousin says there's been a lot of activity in the Borderlands this winter. Last time that happened, we saw raids all through the winter," Ken expounds from his usual table. The guards around him nod in understanding, recalling that his cousin's a Griffin Scout for the

Kingdom. While the guard was a loudmouth, he did not lie about the important things, and orc raiders were definitely important.

Daniel waves to the group, catching the tail of the end of the conversation as he joins them at their table, a mug of beer in his hand. He plops down in his seat with a contented sigh, drawing deep of the beer.

"Good day?" Unusually, it's Curtzman who speaks first after the initial round of greetings as he spots the more relaxed mood the young man is in.

"Yeah, it was. Did very well today. I met a Catkin today, and we worked on clearing the fifth floor together. Finished off quite a few nests," Daniel answers quite proudly. Working with Asin, Daniel had made more today by a significant margin than any previous day, and they hadn't even spent the whole day working together. He couldn't wait for tomorrow. As such, Daniel isn't ready for their reactions.

"Beastkin," one guard spits to the side, the rest grimacing at his choice of companions. More than a few shake their head, their estimation of the young adventurer falling a little.

"What! Why?" Daniel frowns, wondering what is up with his friends.

"Look, we're not prejudiced or anything, Daniel, but, we're guards you know." At Daniel's nod, Ken continues, "Beastkin, well, they make up half our work for being such a small number. Seems like every time we turn around, we're catching another one of their kind and locking them up. They just, well, they're just criminals, most of them. Petty thieves, swindlers, con artists and more. They're either thieves or Adventurers, and the Adventurers aren't much better."

"Just trouble. We should just kick them out," grumbles another red-headed guard.

Daniel frowns, staring at his friends and considers their words. He wasn't a guard, so he couldn't talk about their experiences, but… "She was real helpful to me. Knew where all the traps were and backed me up when I needed it. We made really good time."

Ken holds his hands up placatingly, "I'm sure she's good. There's always a few good ones. Just, you know, the rest of them."

Somewhat mollified, Daniel turns his attention back to his meal despite a part of him being disturbed by the conversation, though the young adventurer is unsure what it is exactly that concerns him.

Chapter 16

The next morning, Asin is surprised to see Daniel waiting for her at the Dungeon entrance, chewing on a loaf of bread and cheese. Since neither of them had thought to arrange a meeting time, Daniel had decided to just get up early and wait for the Catkin. The Catkin slows down for a moment, pulling her cloak tight around her body as she struggles with her feelings. Daniel has been the first human Adventurer who has agreed to and kept his promise of partying up with her again, a fact that stung Asin's pride. Now faced with a human that keeps his word, the Catkin finds herself confused at her own reactions.

The storm of emotion is pushed aside as Daniel finally catches sight of Asin and waves to her, gulping down the mouthful of bread. Asin will test him today, see how he reacts. Even if Daniel worked with Khy'ra, humans were still not to be trusted.

"Morning, Asin." Daniel smiles and stretches. "Are you ready?"

Asin nods in confirmation, hands doing a quick pat down to check that all her weapons and supplies are on-hand. Next to them, the pair of guards who are on night duty watch the Catkin with ill-disguised suspicion. Daniel's eyes narrow slightly, for the first time noticing the guards' reactions. Yet it is not the time to say anything about it as the Catkin strides right past them all, walking into the entrance and heading for the portal stone.

At the stone, she waits for Daniel to catch up before she raises her hand with all her fingers spread to confirm the floor they will work. Daniel nods agreeably and after she has been transported down, places his own hand on the portal stone.

"Cold!" Daniel mutters after checking his surroundings for dangers. Asin can't help but agree with his comment. It always took her a while to get the bone-chilling cold out from her bones. Bent slightly forward, her ears swivel as she listens to the noises coming from the passageways that surround them. There is slight noise coming from two, the third there is none, and in the fourth passageway, she can hear the regular ring of pickaxes on set excrement. That rules out the third and fourth passageways. Prowling to the other two where she hears faint sounds, she sniffs at the air, sorting through the scents before making her final decision.

Daniel watches Asin work without comment, having seen this particular routine a few times already. He marvels at the way her whiskers twitch, sensing the shift in air currents - something that he had to purchase the sage brush for and wave around to notice. It was useful knowledge to have since passageways with higher airflows most likely meant more openings that were available for travel. It was no guarantee, but nothing on these floors was.

As Asin sets off ahead of him, Daniel follows a short distance behind. Neither Adventurer moves quickly, Asin scanning the floor and ceilings for traps, Daniel watching for monsters ahead and behind them as best he can. It is only fifteen minutes in before Asin finds her first trap, a simple deadfall that had been covered by the thinnest level of excrement and dirt. She pauses to point it out to Daniel before moving forwards, leaving Daniel to smash the trap open with his mace. It is only a temporary solution, for a Crawler would be by soon enough to fix it or perhaps even the Dungeon itself would do so.

Scholars still debated how Dungeons fixed traps, and even why traps were present in Dungeons. Many felt the traps were like the monsters, formed out of the corruption in mana by Ba'al. However, that explanation fell short of why Ba'al or the corruption would even bother as traps themselves were inanimate, unlike the monster children of Ba'al. Alternative explanations have risen - that there was not one type of corruption but many and that each type related to a different monster or trap or that the traps themselves were created by another, unseen monster. In the end, the truth was, as far as Daniel could ascertain, no one truly knew, and neither Erlis nor Ba'al was telling.

At the first Crawler they encounter, Asin rushes ahead to fight it alone, ducking beneath the first strike of its mandible to slash with her daggers. The space ahead is too tight for Daniel to join in the battle, not effectively, so he stays behind to watch. Asin's techniques are different from his, relying entirely on speed and precision to cause damage, dodging attacks by inches before lashing out. It makes Daniel feel like a lumbering ox, slow-moving and ungraceful. At least, he comforts himself, her techniques against the Crawler are less effective due to its tough carapace. On the other hand, she must have been a nightmare for the Kobolds to face.

The next Crawler they encounter, Asin smugly hops aside and onto a ledge with a chuffed, "Yours."

Daniel snorts and steps in, bashing the creature with his shield before pounding on the carapace. When the Crawler recovers, its return bite is caught and deflected on his shield and mace, Daniel taking the momentary leverage to kick it with his foot before going back to pounding on it with his mace. The fight is brutal, rough and lacking the finesse of the previous one, but it is shorter.

Panting, Daniel stretches after the fight to force more air into his lungs. Thank Erlis Dungeons somehow circulated their air. Otherwise, it would have been much more difficult to survive this far down. Pushing aside the unnaturalness of it all, Daniel nods again to Asin to continue their exploration.

Fight after fight, cavern after cavern, the two explorers move through the passageways with brutal efficiency. Each trap they find they set off, each monster they kill. It is only when they encounter the Elite of this floor that they pause. A single Elite Crawler, larger than any others with legs tipped with serrated claws, guards the treasure chest.

A shared look is all that is needed before the two Adventurers throw themselves at the monster, both of them knowing what lies in the chest. By now, they've worked out a simple system of fighting. Daniel would stand in front of the monster, keeping the mass of its attention while Asin would work its middle where the creature could not as easily reach her. Against tough opponents, she'd work to cripple the monster, cutting at the legs on one side till it could no longer move.

At first, the battle goes much the same way their previous fights did. Then, in a blink, it changes. As Daniel attempts another Shield Bash, the Elite rears back and clamps its mandibles around the shield. Gripping it tightly, it twists its head and flings Daniel into a wall. He smashes into it, grip lost on the shield which is dropped.

Instead of following after the fallen Adventurer though, the creature turns its attention on Asin, surging in the middle to knock her aside. A leg stabs down, attempting to spear her, cutting a long line across her back as the Catkin rolls away.

Woozy and short-of-breath, Daniel staggers to his feet, Asin scrambling to stay away from the attacks. A dagger flashes out, catching a leg as it attempts to spear her, but before Asin can counter-attack, she has to move again.

Forcing his Gift into his own body, he pulls and rips, fixing the crack in his head and righting the swelling that has begun, pain exploding through his body as he works fast without his usual precautions. No longer injured, Daniel rushes back into the fray with a roar, intent on finishing this battle and repaying the pain he has suffered in spades. The Elite spins back to Daniel, instinctively understanding that the larger Adventurer is the greater threat to its life.

Roaring, Daniel triggers his Double Strike, smashing the first blow into the mandible that comes at him, and following up with a second attack to the same spot. It cracks, and Daniel grabs it tight, pulling down and ripping the mandible off. As the Elite rears back in pain, Asin leaps, climbing swiftly up its back and plunging a knife into an eye. The creature shakes its body, throwing Asin aside into a stalagmite and her body smashes into it with a meaty thump before collapsing in a heap.

Distracted by the attacks and in pain, the Elite feels its own mandible stabbed into its lower body. Unable to keep itself upright, the creature plunges down, impaling itself on the point, driving it deeper. Its chittering takes on a frantic air, its movements erratic, as pain and damage accumulate. Daniel moves away to pick up his discarded shield, stalking the monster as its movements slow and grow less erratic. Once that happens, he moves in to finish the fight.

Under narrowed eyes, Asin watches Daniel finish the Elite. Time to see if he leaves her and takes the crystals. It would be a shame, one that Asin would be sure to return, but better to know now than later. It is to her surprise that Daniel does not do so, instead hurrying to her body —

leaving both crystals unguarded! – to check on her immediately once the Elite bursts into smoke. Warm healing energy fills her body as soon as Daniel nears, bruises and torn muscles knitting swiftly as Daniel chants his Minor Healing spell.

Asin rolls up to her feet, no longer playing at being unconscious and nods her thanks. This one had some Horst then, perhaps more than a little. Asin licks at the fur on the top of her hand as she waves him to pick up the crystals, cleaning away the accumulated dirt. He would do.

Chapter 17

Daniel sighs, stretching and rubbing his left shoulder absently. A crawler had managed to get around his shield and crushed his shoulder earlier today, and though he had healed it with careful application of his Gift and then a Minor Healing spell, it still felt sore. Nothing a good night's rest wouldn't heal, but the pain still crept up on him occasionally.

The door of the Clinic opens again, the next patient enters, and Daniel flashes the man a smile. Asin had requested a short delve today, and so, without anything better to do with his time, Daniel has made his way to the Clinic to provide Khy'ra with some additional help.

"Healer…" the old man shuffles over and sits down, his bare feet unkempt and swollen.

"No healer," Daniel chides softly. He does not have the Healer class and thus will never have access to their specific class skills. He, certainly, is looking forward to reaching Level 10 as an Adventurer and discarding the need for physical baggage as he would gain access to their mystical Inventory class skill.

Even as he thinks these idle thoughts, he is asking questions to ascertain the problem, though it is relatively clear to him. He does not call upon his Gift, seeing no reason to use it in such a simple case. Most of his work in the Clinic was like this in-truth, simple injuries and illnesses that only required non-magical treatment by a knowledgeable healer. Yet, as always, there were few enough people who cared to apply themselves to gather the knowledge and skill to become healers themselves.

"Soak your foot in crushed Wylie leaves. You should be able to get some at Lianne's shop. Make sure she sells you the fresh ones though. Three times a day for a week. A week mind you! If you stop earlier, this will just come back, and you'll have to start again," Daniel says and then makes the man repeat his instructions to him twice before he sends him on his way.

It only takes a minute before the next patient is darkening his doorway, Daniel again absently rubbing at his shoulder. *No time for that, there's always the next patient.*

***

Hours later, Daniel realises it has been a few minutes since a patient has walked into his office. He stands, stretches and groans, wondering how long he has been at this. Darkness fills the room and his stomach clenches in hunger. Well past dinner time at the very least then.

Khy'ra smiles as she enters the doorway, seeing Daniel standing up. The blonde elf is clad in a tight green dress, its plunging neckline hidden behind a white shawl with yellow flowers edging it. She steps in, letting the shawl fall apart as the two are alone, and she smiles at the admiring glances Daniel sends her way.

A swift step takes her to Daniel, and she kisses him tight, moulding her body against his.

Such a pleasure to find a human who didn't tower over her she thinks.

"Hi," Daniel says breathlessly when they break from the kiss.

"Hi," Khy'ra replies, smiling up at him but not moving from his arms. "I've sent the staff home for the evening. So if we're quiet…"

Daniel grins, not needing another reply and picks her up, walking to the nearby table. Such a pleasure to find a human of her height who was so strong amends Khy'ra. Then she's not thinking much of anything for a while.

***

Stomach rumbling, Daniel pulls his pants up and looks at Khy'ra who comes back from the restroom, "Care for dinner?"

"Yes, I do believe so," Khy'ra says, leaning forwards and kissing him. "Your technique is improving."

Daniel grunts, pulling her closer and mutters, "You know, that's not what most men want to hear."

"You do though," she giggles and taps his nose. "It's what I like about you, Daniel, you're quite willing to listen to instruction."

Daniel snorts and gives her another kiss before letting her go. "Come on, let's get some food."

Outside, after locking up, the two walk down the lightly illuminated streets. At night, few are out to walk the streets. In this part of town, the mana lantern crystals are interspersed at great distances, making both of their shadows stretch out before them. The two chat quietly, nodding in greeting as a pair of guards walks past them on patrol.

"Khy'ra, Daniel! Good to see you!" Mikey, the owner, calls out and waves them into a pair of free seats. As the closest late night dining establishment to the Clinic, he is not at all surprised to see the two. "Late night again?"

"Two plates for me, Mikey!" Daniel calls out as he sits down.

"The usual," Khy'ra adds.

Seated, Khy'ra takes Daniel's arms in hers while they both turn to watch Mikey work. Mikey first takes a scoop of batter, ladling it into the oval, scooped cooking pans before him, swirling the batter around as he works them in. A quick flick of his hand ensures that the batter covers everything properly on each of the pans that he starts before he turns around. Hands pick up knives and flicker, slicing off thin slices of meat from the roast that rotates behind him. Slices, perfectly sized all are placed on the thinly applied, already cooked bread. Hands dance then as cheese, slices of red pepper, cucumbers and mushrooms are added before the bread is rolled together. Each roll is then quickly slid into a small oven, the cheese and entire dish toasted for just a minute before the rolls are ready.

Khy'ra and Daniel enjoy the show; Mikey is a known master of his craft. Even as he gets their order ready, he begins others, constantly moving to ensure that none of his plates are ever over-cooked. Business, even this late, is always busy at his location.

When dinner arrives with a thump, the two dig-in with gusto, blowing hard at the rolls and huffing around too-hot mouthfuls. Eyes crinkling in amusement at each other's antics, the two lovers only stop when bells begin to ring throughout the town.

Daniel pauses, tilting his head to the side, never having heard these particular bells before. Next to him, Khy'ra has her head hung down, whispering a soft prayer. "QuanEr, for pain, peace. For anger, forgiveness. For hatred, love."

It is only when he hears Khy'ra's prayer that Daniel knows what the bells are for, and he too hangs his head, repeating the prayer. It is no surprise, for all the myriad gods that meddle in mortal life, only one is revered through all the lands. She who rose from humanity like many others, but who refused to ascend. She who walked among mortals still, providing aid and care without price, without cost, without judgement. Once a year, bells are rung and remembrance given to QuanEr throughout the lands.

Silence reigns before Mikey lets out a little yelp, and his carefully orchestrated dance of food preparation is broken. Muttering, he tosses the burnt food aside amongst the others that will go to those less fortunate later on before restarting his work.

Dinner is soon finished by the two famished healers, and they quietly deposit the plates and money on the counter next to Mikey. As they walk, Khy'ra notices Daniel rubbing his shoulder again and places a hand on it, murmuring a soft chant to complete the healing process. Idiot must have used the last of his mana earlier in the day.

"Thanks," Daniel repeats, and Khy'ra just shakes her head, leaning her head on his shoulder as they head back to her apartment by unspoken consent.

Chapter 18

Months later, spring has finally arrived. The snow has melted, the sun arriving earlier and earlier each day. With the setting this evening, Daniel and Asin are back in the Adventurer's Guild, collecting another day's earnings. As usual, Asin is taking care of this, leaving Daniel to wander around the Guild Hall till she is done.

"Liev, what's this?" Daniel points to the appearance of the new board in the Guild Hall. It's obviously been moved, and after a moment's recollection, Daniel remembers seeing it in the far corner previously. The board stands to the side of the attendant booths, positioned such that Adventurers may peruse the board without blocking access to the booths themselves.

"It's the request board. Now that spring's here, we're getting more and more requests for Adventurers to help around the town and surrounding villages. We move it up every spring, since during the winter it's mostly Quests for more advanced Adventurers," Liev explains, looking up from the papers he is working on. The redhead runs a hand through his hair, messing it up even further as he purses his lips, trying to decipher the handwriting before him. Liev would curse the writer, if the writer were not him. Instead, he reminds himself to take notes with more care. As Liev finishes speaking, Asin comes up next to Daniel and hands him his share silently before joining Daniel in staring at the board. It takes her a moment to let out a chuff and turn back to licking at the black fur on top of her hands.

Having received his answer, Daniel turns back to study the board in more detail with renewed interest. The board itself is split into four parts with a carving above each portion indicating the type of request it was, with a simple rating system consisting of the Guild's seal beneath each portion in ascending order of difficulty. A single seal meant the quest was suitable for Beginner Adventurers, with up to four stamps being the highest on the current board. That one consisted of a request to hunt a manticore which had taken residence in the Borderlands near a village. The four categories showcased were for Hunt, Supply, and Guard quests with a final miscellaneous section that currently consists of numerous scouting and exploration requests. Each Quest had a written portion that detailed the quest and a simply drawn image below it for those who couldn't read, allowing most Adventurers a quick idea of what each quest entailed.

Daniel quickly relays his findings to Asin who nods her head at the words before pointing to the Hunt and, with a slight hesitation, the Supply portions of the board. Preference offered, Daniel turns back to the board to search for an appropriate Quest. After spending the entire winter working the Dungeon, a change of pace was called for.

"Liev, what's the circle for?" Daniel points to a notation that he has spotted that appears more regularly on the Supply side than the Hunt sections.

"Repeatable quests. Most unique quests require a deposit by the Adventurer and have a time limit. The repeatable ones don't since multiple Adventurers can work on them at the same time. Most of those quests are from traders looking for new material, though the Guard, of course, have their regular bounties on Orcs, Goblins and Kobolds," Liev clarifies.

"These two are in the North of Karlak and are around the same area, I think. 40 Silver each," Daniel points and Asin looks up for a brief moment, considering the pieces of paper before an eloquent shrug provides her answer.

Daniel sighs, having gotten used to the ever-eloquent nature of his friend and party member after many weeks of working with her. He pulls the papers down and walks over to Liev. A change of pace would be nice after being stuck on the fifth floor for weeks, crawling through passageways and fighting the same monsters again and again. Twice before, the two had attempted the sixth floor out of frustration, and both times they had found fighting on that floor too difficult. The Behemoth Crawlers that inhabited the floor were not only larger than their upper floor brethren, their armour was significantly tougher, and it took both Adventurers working until exhaustion to kill even one.

"That's 40 Silver then." Liev takes the two papers, glad for the momentary distraction from his paperwork and looks at Daniel whose jaw has dropped. Liev just smiles, knowing the two Adventurers between them have enough - they did just pay them out for the day.

Grumbling to himself, Daniel casts a beseeching look to Asin who hands over her portion too before they receive confirmation that they are now assigned to the requests with a three-day completion requirement.

***

"This is rather nice, isn't it?" Daniel makes conversation the next morning as they head out of the North gate. Asin provides the unspoken agreement by running ahead of him and then squatting down to grab a handful of newly bloomed flowers in her hands, the yellow and pink flowers contrasting with her black fur. She sniffs them and then slides one into her brooch before offering the other to Daniel.

A shake of his head makes her wrinkle her nose, her whiskers bouncing around at the motion before she drops the flower and joins Daniel as he walks.

"So, we've got to find a Shadow Cat and an Owlbear that have come too close to town and are threatening the farmers in the area," Daniel muses before glancing at his companion. "Do you have any tracking skills?"

Asin pauses, tilting her head up she sniffs disdainfully at Daniel and then continues.

"Is that a yes?" Daniel queries, and not getting an answer, hurries up to catch up with her. He's hoping that's a yes. It is a 40 silver deposit they've put down already, and while he has some minor experience in the woods himself, he would not call himself a tracker. When he asks again, all he gets is silence, so he lets the topic drop. The rest of the walk is finished in companionable silence, both parties enjoying the nice change of pace as the Spring sun shines down on them with the just the barest hint of cold in the air from the night before.

The pair has walked for hours, taking them from the outskirts of the city where farmers work towards the edge of the settled lands that border Karlak. Here, gently rolling hills dotted with large farms worked by dedicated farmers have transformed into smaller farms where pioneers work to build their lives. Many of the farms in this part of the world are small, the space between each farm large, and most are threadbare in their fittings with a single building. Many of these farmers stabled their animals in their houses themselves, both as a safety precaution and to add additional heat to their dwellings. Now, with the snow gone, they are hard at work felling new trees for fences, wood and just to extend their plots.

"This is where the quest says the Cat was last seen." Daniel gestures around the forest, which just gets another disdainful sniff from Asin. Using the map provided by Liev at the Guild and his

Mapping proficiency, Daniel has been able to guide them to the appropriate spot unerringly.

Asin prowls away from Daniel, walking in a slow circle as she stares at the ground and occasionally sniffs at the air, taking over now that they are close to the monster. Daniel sighs and falls silent, letting her get to work as he pulls his shield off his back.

It's a few minutes later when she gestures for him to follow. The two begin walking into the woods, Daniel following after Asin when she turns and points to his feet and then her ears, hissing at him in disapproval. Daniel grimaces and tries to walk quieter, though the glare he gets from the absolutely silent Catkin tells him how well he is doing.

After a few hours, Daniel realises there is a reason why these quests paid so well - spending hours tramping through the woods not killing anything was significantly less interesting than the Dungeon itself. For Adventurers who craved excitement and adventure, tramping through the undergrowth was less than rewarding. Thankfully, Asin seems to know what she is doing, or at least she seems confident, extremely confident to Daniel, as she follows a trail that only she is able to see.

Unfortunately for them, a certain city dweller's heavy feet have given their prey more than sufficient warning. The Shadow Cat has doubled back, crawling up a large oak tree and crouches on it, waiting for its prey to arrive. Watching the two cross below it, the Cat decides to attack the larger of the two and launches itself from its perch, smashing into Daniel with its claws. One claw catches on Daniel's shield, the other on his armour as the beast knocks him to the ground. Claws rip into him, and a paw rises to finish the foolish Adventurer.

The paw never completes its journey, a thrown knife slamming into the fast-moving limb. Hurt and angered, the Cat shifts to snarl at its new assailant which gives Daniel enough time and leverage to throw it off his body with a heave. Rolling back onto his knees, Daniel throws a clumsy and hasty swipe of his mace to force the Cat to back off. The Cat lands on its injured paw, hissing in pain as the blade drives deeper and Daniel is able to stand fully and bring his shield up on guard, bloodied but alive.

The Cat lets out a low rumbling growl, assessing the two creatures before it, taking careful steps backward into the shadows that surround the trees above it. A second knife tumbles through the air, but the Cat is gone, fading into the shadows before their eyes. Daniel moves to place a nearby tree to his back, shield held up to guard himself, and Asin moves to join him, both Adventurers awaiting the next attack. No attacks come, and after a time, Daniel squats to begin healing the deep cuts in his back and across the back of his head as Asin moves around the clearing carefully to see if she can pick up traces of the creature. When Daniel has finished healing himself, she beckons him over, pointing to the trail of blood that she has found.

Together, the two follow the trail, eyes peeled for danger. After an hour of careful navigation, they come across a slow-moving river where the trail stops. Snarling in anger, Asin moves up and down the river and even crosses it, attempting to pick up the trail again but is unable to do so. The Cat is gone and hours of further searching yields no further result. Disappointed, they make camp for the evening and, realising that they no longer have a lead, decide to switch targets to the Owlbear. Perhaps the Cat will make itself known while they deal with the Owlbear.

Chapter 19

The Owlbear's lair is a simple cave hidden in a depression surrounded by trees, the perfect place for the creature. Outside, there are scattered bones from its recent meals of stolen sheep and the larger bones of a bear - the cave's former occupant. For a time, the pair of Adventurers watch the Owlbear's cave to ensure the monster is alone before ascertaining their plan. Of course, since neither are tactical geniuses, their plan is simplistic in the utmost.

Daniel moves to the depression, shield and mace at the ready. Once he's set, he strikes the mace against his shield boss, drawing the creature out. The strikes are loud in the forest, drawing the ire of the monster. When the Owlbear lumbers out, Daniel pales at the sight of the nine-foot-tall feathered monstrosity whose front limbs end in paws instead of eagle claws. Yet, the humanoid body structure and face itself is that of a bear, with only vestigial wings at its back.

As the Owlbear roars, daggers flash forward one after the other to sink into the creature's flesh. The blades are targeted to the creature's softer underbelly, the Owlbear's tiny inset eyes too difficult a throw for the hidden Asin. Instead, she goes for quantity over quality, injuring the creature and distracting it as Daniel rushes forward.

Ducking beneath the first paw strike, Daniel targets a knife that is stuck in the creature's body and drives it deeper with his blow. He keeps moving, getting out of range of the return attack, forcing the Owlbear to turn to chase him. Another knife flashes out, taking the creature in the back but failing to draw its attention away from Daniel.

Daniel ducks the first lurching strike and blocks the second on his shield, using the opening to smash against the claw. The Owlbear hisses, ducking forwards with its head to bite Daniel. Fetid breath from rotting flesh stuck in its teeth misses Daniel by inches as he ducks to the side, swinging a backhanded strike to the creature's muzzles. The combatants are too close for thrown weapons now, so Asin instead rushes forwards on silent feet and launches herself with daggers extended, landing on the monster's back and allowing her own clawed feet and daggers to dig into the monster.

The creature roars in anger and rears back, the Owlbear's claws unable to reach its new assailant. Daniel matches the roar, raising his mace high to smash down with all his strength on the creature's exposed chest. The Owlbear's bones are surprisingly brittle, and Daniels mace sinks deep into the creature's chest. The unexpected lack of resistance forces Daniel off-balance for a brief moment and a rotating claw catches him high up on his shoulder, ripping muscles and tendons apart as Daniel loses grip of his weapon.

Daniel stumbles away, catching the next strike by reflex on his shield but is sent sprawling to the ground. Behind, Asin uses the dagger to repeatedly stab the monster in its neck, who gurgles as blood rushes into its throat. In a desperate attempt to kill at least one of its assailants, it stomps down at Daniel who rolls away, the attack tearing his back open. Strength finally gone, the Owlbear collapses forwards, forcing Asin to throw herself into a roll to escape harm.

Daniel groans, lying on his back and focusing on healing his wounds with his mana. The monster's claws were sharp and the creature strong, shredding the hardened leather armour on his back as if it was paper. "Why am I the one who always gets hit?"

Asin does her version of a laugh, chuffing as she takes the loot from the monster. She points to herself as she finishes pocketing the mana stone and claws, "Fast. Smart." Her hands come up to point at Daniel, and she finishes, "Strong. Slow."

Daniel snorts, rotating his shoulder as he finishes healing and stands up. "You're just using me as a meat shield."

She chuffs more and then points back into the woods before continuing, "Cat?"

Daniel nods, heading back to their backpacks, "Yeah. Though I think we need a new plan."

She nods in agreement, jade eyes narrowing as she remembers how the Shadow Cat had counter stalked them and managed to run away even with one of her daggers in its paw. She really liked that dagger too.

***

A couple of days later, the two are standing in the Guild Hall, handing in the Owlbear's claws as proof of their success. They are dejected, however, as their various plans to deal with the Shadow Cat - from using bait to laying crudely built traps - were a failure. It is only on the last day when they are heading back do they hear of a good lead but by then, it is too late. Only once more did they come across a pair of tracks, but Asin had waved them off, fearing that the creature was likely luring them into a trap again.

"Cat got the better of you?" Liev chuckles softly, handing them their pay and half their deposit back. The glum nods make Liev chuckle. "It's okay, those things are tough. Really, Rangers are the only ones who stand a chance finding those Cats."

"You could have told us that earlier," Daniel mentally groans but when he takes the coins, he has to smile at the new pop-up.

Quest Completed
Hunt the Owlbear (1 / 1)
2,000 XP Received

Level Up!
Adventurer Level 5
You have gained 5 attribute points

As the happy purr from Asin attests, she probably received the same Quest completion. *Well*, Daniel thinks, *there might be at least one other reason to complete Quests.*

***

With a little bit of time on his hands, Daniel walks into the training grounds for the first time in months, marvelling at how little the grounds had changed in the intervening period. The same old smell of sweating bodies, oil and metal fill the air, and the same grunts and occasional groans of pain or frustration.

He waves to Litzburn, who breaks out into a wide smile before making a last few comments to his current students before walking to Daniel. They share a quick handclasp, Litzburn looking over his old student with a practised eye. Daniel had put on even more muscles than before, though the way he held himself spoke of a better sense of his own body as well. The slight tilt of his body to where the combatants were, told of a new wariness the novice youngster had previously lacked. Overall, Litzburn was satisfied — the young man was coming along well. Of course, he couldn't let the youngster know that. "You need a haircut."

Chuckling, Daniel runs a hand through his brown mop of hair and nods, "Yeah, got to get that done."

"Well, go get ready then," Litzburn pushes him to the walls where the training weapons are. "Floor 3."

Daniel nods happily, hurrying off to get the training gear. When he arrives back on the floor, he's surprised to see Litzburn casually stretching, light glinting off his oiled bald head. For a moment Daniel feels trepidation, before he grins, realising this is a great chance to see how far he has come.

The moment Litzburn nods his readiness, Daniel launches an attack, stepping forwards and using Double Strike. Litzburn blocks the first, dodges the second, and has to skip backwards slightly to avoid the Shield Bash that comes his way next. Daniel does not let up, pushing the tempo of the fight to keep the more experienced fighter off-balance. Litzburn continues to block each strike with minimal motion, batting Daniel's mace aside and forcing wider and wider strikes before he lunges, having created the opening he was looking for. Struck full in the chest, Daniel stumbles back, his breath forced from his body.

"Hold!"

Daniel nods in thanks, getting his breath back as Litzburn walks forward. "Good. You're faster and stronger, and you kept up the training yourself, didn't you? Your basics are solid."

Daniel grumbles, "Didn't hit you though."

"No. You're too direct, no real feints. That's fine against dumb monsters, but against smarter opponents, you need to create the openings you need." Watching Daniel he continues, "There are two major kinds of feints – movement and attack feints. You can feint by committing to a movement and then shifting." Litzburn showcases it, shifting his weight to the front foot, his entire body angling to the right before bouncing to the left.

"Or you can feint an attack, forcing the opponent to create an opening. Feints are all about making the opponent move, but they don't work if you aren't seen to commit. A feinted attack should look, should feel, like a real attack." Litzburn lips twist in wry amusement. "Or you can just attack and change it mid-way like Mary."

Daniel absorbs the information in silence, before raising his mace once more. Litzburn steps back, and they begin. Almost bored, Litzburn adds as they fight, "Don't fall into a pattern either, especially of using your special attacks. A smart opponent will see it and do something like THIS!"

Litzburn blocks the Shield Bash, and then wraps Daniel's shield and arm with his own before Daniel can pull back. A quick step puts Litzburn inside Daniel's defence as he begins to pull Daniel downwards, stretching the shorter Adventurer over his knee. Free hand raised, it flashes towards Daniel's neck and stops at the last moment, completing the demonstration.

"Now, let's begin again."

Chapter 20

"This way!" Khy'ra pulls on Daniel's arm, dragging him down the pathway, blonde hair flowing in the wind. He smiles, enjoying the view as the elf in the light summer dress hurries along, wind pushing the dress against her body, hugging her full curves. It is a touch chilly, a last-minute frost the night before slowly thawing in the spring sun.

"Come on, Khy'ra." Daniel laughs, shaking his head, "You told me to take a day off, and now you're dragging me around. It's not like I don't mind taking a day off, but couldn't we spend some time actually resting?"

She snorts, turning around and waiting for him to catch up before kissing him on his nose. "Sex later."

Daniel blushes slightly, still uncomfortable by the frank way Khy'ra deals with certain topics. "I didn't mean that!"

"Of course you didn't." She grins, pulling him on. "Anyway, the only reason you agreed to come was that Asin refused to work again today. I believe she eloquently put it as you being work stupid."

Looking ahead, all that Daniel can see as a potential destination is a small hut at the end of the curved pathway, the only apparent structure among the rolling green hills that they traverse. He ignores hers and Asin's pointed comments, knowing they were correct and that he could get a touch focused at times. However, they just needed to level up and then maybe they'd be able to deal with the next floor. Just a little bit more. "Are you really not going to tell me what this is about?"

"Patience!"

As they near the hut, Daniel notes that the clothing line outside seems to be built on a small pulley to raise and lower it. The hut itself looks to be relatively well kept, no obvious holes and the thatched roof recently redone. Khy'ra does not wait to knock on the door, instead stepping in directly. The inside of the hut is a contrast to the neat external and is a complete mess with tables filling up every inch of space and laden down with a wide array of items - shields, swords, maces, jewellery and more. In a rare clear space on the table in the centre of the room, a series of etching tools and a small beaker sit, containers filled with copper, silver and gold dust next to it.

"Khy'ra, lass, you made it!" A low voice rumbles from the kitchen, soon followed by its owner. The dwarf whose residence this is comes out from the kitchen holding a frying pan and wearing an apron, his full brown beard braided to remove itself from danger. Brown eyes twinkle as he hefts the pan, slabs of heavenly smelling bacon roasting on it, setting Daniel's starving stomach clenching.

"Tharuk, boy, I told you I'd be here today," Khy'ra says, stepping into the hut and pointing behind to Daniel. "This is Daniel; he's a friend."

"Tharuk. That smells amazing." Daniel greets the dwarf and then angles for an invitation.

Tharuk laughs, leading the way into the kitchen, "Come. There's more than enough for everybody!"

A short thirty minutes later, Daniel is patting his stomach having stuffed himself. *Tharuk was definitely a very good cook, better he would say than even Elise, though he knew better than to ever say that!* "That was wonderful, Tharuk. Thank you. I'm now glad Khy'ra dragged me out here."

"Any friend of the lass is a friend of mine." Tharuk grins, standing up to begin putting away the dishes. "Even if he's stolen her away from me."

Daniel blanches and shoots a look at Khy'ra who just smiles blandly at him. Tharuk seems to be missing the awkwardness his words have created, coming back and offering further nourishment. "Cake?"

"Uhh…," Daniel stares at the cake and then shrugs, taking the plate. "Thank you."

"The lass says you've been having trouble with the sixth floor?" Tharuk mentions around his mouthful of cake. Khy'ra stays silent, savouring her own piece as she lets the two talk.

"Yes. The Behemoth Crawlers are just too strong. We can kill one, but it takes forever, and if there are two, we just have to run away," Daniel grumbles, waving his fork around. "There's always a few of them in a nest at a time, and I don't even want to think what the boss is like."

"The Crawlers are horrible. Tough carapace makes it nearly impossible to smash through or stab. Most Adventurers have to level up a few times or party up enough to beat the floor. Khy'ra says you're too impatient for that though, got places to be and all that."

"Well, I'm… you know…" Daniel grimaces, shrugging his shoulders.

"Young." Tharuk laughs heartily and points to the front of his hut and his workshop as he finishes up his cake. "Alright, I got something that can help. You and your Catkin."

Walking past Daniel, he pushes the Adventurer down as he tries to stand up to follow. A few minutes later, Tharuk returns with two pairs of bracers with etchings inlaid in copper on them. "Normally, I don't work with such low materials these days, but I couldn't say no to Khy'ra."

"What are they?" Daniel picks one up, frowning at the etchings. There's something about the bracers, a feeling of power that he can sense at the edges of his perception. He extends his senses a bit further, feeling the bracers through his mana and realising that the bracers seem to contain and hold mana themselves. "These are enchanted!"

Lesser Braces of Lightning
Effect: When worn, Braces add 3 — 5 Points of Lightning Damage per successful attack. 5% chance to stun (resisted by Magic Resistance).
Durability: 30/30
Item Class: Enchanted
Quality: Excellent (+2 to Enchantment Damage)

"Well, I am an enchanter." Tharuk gestures to the bracers before him, smiling slightly in pride. "These are enchanted with lightning magic. If you wear them, your aura will be imbued with lightning magic itself, and each of your attacks will do a small portion of lightning damage. The Crawlers themselves are susceptible, so you'll be able to kill them a lot easier."

Daniel's grin widens even further as he caresses the bracers. "Thank you!"

"You are very welcome. I'll also need 12 Gold for the bracer sets," Tharuk states. Daniel's jaw drops open, the sheer amount staggering. A thrifty man could survive on a single gold for a year; twelve was a fortune. "Each."

Suddenly, the heavenly brunch he ate feels like lead in his stomach. He had been earning a decent amount for a while now, but still. "I uhh… don't have that much."

"Of course not. Just give the money to Khy'ra when you can. I trust you!" Khy'ra just smiles, raising her cup as Daniel reels from the news. This was his first enchanted item, but for so much. He pushes down the feelings of trepidation. He always knew that being an Adventurer was an expensive proposition; it seemed it was time for him to truly decide. Would he strive for the top or become just another low-tier Adventurer, working small-time dungeons and earning enough to have a comfortable, but unexciting life.

Put that way, there really was little choice. If Daniel had wanted comfort, he had simpler, easier options, "Thank you. I'll repay you as soon as I can. We will."

Unable to stop himself, Daniel quickly straps the bracers on. The moment both are equipped, a surge of energy ripples through him, invading his aura. Concentrating, he can feel the flickers of lightning mana that are now imbued into his aura, stretching forth to cover him. As he picks up a fork, he can feel how it flows down even to the fork, charging it with a slight measure of the lightning mana and his own aura. The two old friends just watch as he plays with his new toy, sharing knowing smiles.

***

"Mrs. Hearth, what did we say about overdoing it?" Daniel grumbles later that evening, raising the elderly woman's arm to inspect it again and then letting it drop.

The octogenarian cackles for a moment before wincing in pain, "Young man, at my age, you take what time you get and make full use of it."

Snorting, Daniel sighs and reaches out with his Gift, slowly reknitting the torn tendons and muscles in the shoulder. Healing in this way was old hat to Daniel by now, though with Khy'ra's guidance, he had learnt to use less power, making smaller adjustments to allow the body's natural healing abilities to take over. However, his biggest gains in skill were when he helped the diseased and the elderly, their various ailments and illnesses outside of his previous experience in the mining camps. The hard life of the camp was no place for the weak or elderly, so what he mostly treated were injuries, not the common ailments he dealt with now.

Finished with the old woman, he sends her out before turning to Khy'ra who has wandered in. After exchanging a quick kiss, she announces, "That's it for the day. Thank you for coming in with me, Daniel, I felt bad about taking the morning off."

Daniel just nods, accepting the thanks gracefully. It wasn't exactly what he would consider a rest day but who was he to complain, "Khy'ra, one question."

"Mmm…?"

"I've noticed some of the patients, well, they seem to refuse to go to you." He gestures to the now empty waiting room.

"Oh, mmm… not refuse. They're just more comfortable with you," Khy'ra explains, looking over to the youngster.

"Right…" Daniel's eyes narrow before he flinches as Khy'ra punches him in the arm.

"Don't," she warns him, and he sighs, nodding. No point making a fuss about it, even if their actions just made no sense. As his grandfather pointed out, fools would be fools. Still, he might make those wait a little longer next time and use more traditional methods with them. No point in wasting his gift for those…

"Ow!"

"I said, don't." Khy'ra holds her fist up, glaring at Daniel before he nods quickly.

"No fuss, no fuss."

"Good. I much prefer being hit…" Khy'ra grins lasciviously at the suddenly blushing Daniel. He still rejoins, however.

"You do, do you…"

Chapter 21

"This."

Smash.

"Is."

Smash.

"Awesome!"

Smash.

Lightning dances again as Daniel's mace crushes the Behemoth Crawler. The creature shudders again, the lightning piercing through its shattered carapace. It doesn't go down easy though, swinging its head around to strike at Daniel with its mandibles. The jerky attack is caught easily on Daniel's shield though, and its body is levered up long enough for Daniel to swing an underhand blow to its thinner under-armour. The Crawler shudders once more and falls dead, allowing Daniel to survey the rest of the nest on the sixth floor.

To his right, Asin is throwing knife after knife into the squirming mass of junior Crawlers. They struggle to get to her, but as they close she lightly leaps away and continues her attack. As each strike hits, the tell-tale flicker of lightning arrives, shocking the crawlers. Asin switches targets as one Crawler gets too close, twisting the knife in her hand and sending it into a spiralling movement as she activates her skill proficiency, Piercing Throw. The newly imbued knife shatters the carapace as it lands, lightning mana doing further damage inside the unprotected flesh. Through experimentation, the novice

Adventurers have learnt that Asin's knives hold the enchantment for a short distance before fading away, though imbuing the knives with her Skill Proficiencies aided in extending the range.

As the injured Crawler finally manages to close the distance, Asin backflips out of the way, her trailing foot kicking the Crawler in the face as one last spiteful farewell, lightning dancing as the blow lands to kill the creature. Daniel enters the fray then, his mace making quick work of the last few wounded junior Crawlers. As they loot the bodies, neither Adventurer can hide their glee at the speed they completed this nest.

"So…." Daniel tilts his head to Asin, hefting his mace and trying to sound professional. "Boss?"

The Catkin in her usual crouch looks up at Daniel, wrinkling her muzzle though her eyes sparkle as well. She takes a moment to act like she's thinking about it but her mind is already made up as she nods firmly.

Unfortunately, actually finding the Boss in the sixth level was a chore in itself. Nearly half as large again as the fifth floor, the two Adventurers have to call it a day before they are able to locate its lair. Even with Daniel occasionally wiping their fatigue away with his Gift, he could do nothing about the mental exhaustion of crawling through the dark in constant danger.

They have no luck either for the next three days, and on the fourth, they arrive too late as another party finishes the monstrous Crawler off just minutes before they arrive. Glumly, the pair leaves the celebrating party to their spoils, knowing the Boss would likely respawn in a new location. The only major gain during the last few days was that they had found the stairs down to the seventh floor where they registered themselves but did not explore.

"I'm feeling lucky today!" Daniel states as they transfer down to the sixth floor once again. Asin just chuffs, having heard this pronouncement four times already, though she is as excited as to get this done as he is. However, this time, he speaks the truth as they come across the sixth floor's boss after only a few hours of searching and just a single fight with a nest.

As Mary had initially mentioned, the boss in the Dungeon was of the same form as the other monsters before it, just more powerful. Having seen the corpse of the boss before, neither Adventurer is surprised at the Titanic Crawler's size, but a part of them still wonders how it managed to make its way around the tight tunnels of the sixth floor.

The Titanic Crawler was twice the size of a Behemoth Crawler, its head alone four and a half feet wide. Its body stretched behind it, curled up in what looked to be sleep and stumping their guesses, though it was at least twenty feet long. Its carapace gleamed darkly in the faint light, the creature resting while its prey searched for it.

The two do not need to speak, having worked out sure-fire tactics when dealing with a single enemy. Asin enters first, silent as only a Catkin could be and quickly clambers up a wall, putting herself out of danger. Hidden in the shadows, she readies her attacks and begins the battle with a Piercing Throw. She follows up immediately with another, targeting the same spot in the middle of the back, looking to shatter the carapace. Too far away for the bracers enchantments to work, the shots still shatter the carapace in small chunks, sufficient to allow the knives following to land in unprotected flesh.

The Crawler roars, shaking the cavern as it comes under attack and rears towards Asin's newly revealed presence. Daniel takes advantage of this, charging the creature to Shield Bash it. The creature stumbles back, lightning dancing as Daniel proceeds to target the legs on one side to cripple the Boss's movements.

It is only two blows in, a single leg among multitudes shattered before the Crawler spins, using its bulk to smash against Daniel. He brings his hands up together in time to block, using both his Shield and mace to support his block. Safe the from the immediate retaliation, Daniel begins to hammer at the creature, keeping it focused on him as Asin drops from the ceiling and runs the creature's length to reach her embedded knives. Once there, she begins tearing at the shattered carapace to get at the unprotected flesh inside.

The Boss thrashes, attempting to throw Asin off while simultaneously trying to crush Daniel with his mandibles. Daniel fights defensively, foiling attacks against him and only lashing out when he can to send sparks of lightning damage against the monster. The repeated bashings, it seems, have hardly slowed it; as Asin finally creates an opening wide enough for her own liking, she plunges her knife into its back.

The Titanic Crawler then does something unexpected, rolling over entirely. The Catkin throws herself off, but the momentary surprise means that she is unable to leap clear of the body entirely. The Titanic Crawler's bulk lands on her legs, forcing a choked scream from her.

Daniel leaps, using both arms to swing his mace at the softer carapace that the Crawler has exposed. The blows force the creature to roll again to protect its body, a foot spearing Asin in the stomach as it does so. She lets out a choked groan, pain radiating from her broken feet but the Catkin pushes past it, chopping at the leg with her knife to free herself. Once she is able to do so, she begins to pull herself away from the monster, letting out choked off whimpers of pain with each movement.

Luckily, Daniel has the creature's attention now, allowing Asin to crawl away as he triggers his proficiencies, again and again, battering at the creature to keep its attention. He can feel the strength of his blows slowing, fatigue catching up as he attacks and dodges in a desperate attempt to save his friend. Finally, a lucky Shield Bash stuns the creature for a few seconds, allowing Daniel to run and grab his teammate to escape into a nearby tunnel shaft.

Inside the smaller tunnel, safe for the moment, Daniel spins around to focus on healing his teammate. He doesn't need his Gift to tell she is gravely injured, both her legs shattered by the weight of the behemoth and the Crawler's leg still sticking from her stomach.

Focused, he pushes his Gift out even as he extracts the leg and begins to rearrange her leg bones manually. Asin chokes back a quick scream before falling unconscious from the pain as Daniel sets her bones with quick, efficient movements. His Gift begins to take from him almost immediately, pulling memories of previous battles, stretching muscles and nerves as it strips it of their gained experience to fuel the healing. What feels like days later as memories and experience both good and bad disappear, Daniel comes to from his trance and slumps next to his friend.

He shudders, his body slowly accustoming itself to its new state. Asin is awake by the time he is fully aware, staring at her healed body with awe. She points to him, and Daniel just nods, and she chuffs out, a low rumble coming from her. Still not having learnt to speak Catkin, Daniel just shrugs and forces himself to stand up.

"You know, I bet that Boss hasn't healed yet…" Daniel muses, his mace slapping into his hand.

The agreeable yowl from Asin indicates her agreement and Daniel's face tightens into a grim smile. Time to get some experience back.

***

"Ugh…" Daniel shakes the remnant of his shield loose, tossing it to the side in disgust. The Crawler had attempted its smashing move again, this time dropping its weight on Daniel. Unfortunately for the Crawler, it hadn't expected the Adventurer to just block it, the strong ex-miner catching the full force on his extended shield arm and just about able to hold it off the ground. The mistake was fatal for the already wounded creature, Asin sliding underneath to savage the creature from beneath and pierce its three hearts.

The creature dead, its body dissolving, the two Adventurers rest for a few moments before they move to pick up the Boss's chemical sac and mana stone before walking to the chest. Inside, they grin at the largest mana stone either has seen, glowing with clear light.

Now, this is a real stone, Daniel thinks, picking it up to admire it. Asin purrs for a moment, and then her face closes down, looking between the stone and Daniel. She then points to him and states, "Yours."

"Huh?" Pulled from his greedy contemplation, Daniel shakes his head at her implication. "Ours."

"Yours." Insists Asin, now pushing at his arm to make the stone get closer to Daniel.

"No. Ours." Daniel pauses, realising he's falling into the rhythm of her speech again. "This is ours. We're partners. You save me, I save you. That's the way this works."

Asin chuffs, letting out a low growl and pushes again at the stone. "Yours."

"No." The two then exchange glares, eyes locked in a contest of wills that neither wants to give up. The tense silence hovers around them for long minutes, neither willing to look away or give in. It is only the sound of approaching Crawlers that make the two break their gazes. Daniel glares at her one last time then shrugs, tossing the stone back into the chest.

"Fine. No one's then," Daniel grumbles, turning to walk towards the incoming monsters. If they weren't taking the stone, at least he could start making some money back from the other Crawlers.

Asin just stands there shocked at this frustrating human, a low rumbling growl in Catkin arising from her throat. That was money he was throwing away, a lot of it! *Why would he not let her show her gratitude for saving her life?* Frustrated and unhappy that she lost, she grabs the stone out from the chest again and scrambles after him. *At least she wasn't willing to leave good money behind to make a point.*

Chapter 22

"You two should talk," Liev says to Daniel as he waits around for Asin to finish up with their day's take.

"I don't know what you're talking about," Daniel replies, looking back to Liev and the older attendant sniffs, running a hand through the curly mess of his hair again.

"You two are having problems. It's affecting your work. I've seen the tally for the last few days, and you two are down. And it's not just the shorter hours you are working either," Liev says and raises a finger. "Though that's part of it. I've never seen you or her out of the Dungeon before eight bells two days in a row before, and this is the fourth day you are both here."

Daniel crosses his arms, replying, "You all keep saying I should take a break, maybe that's what we're doing."

"Is it?" Liev reiterates, and Daniel shifts uncomfortably, looking away from the attendant. "I thought so. Talk."

Standing up, Liev walks away, and Daniel sighs. Liev was right, the past few days, the uncomfortable silence between the two Adventurers after their first real fight had affected their teamwork, and the unspoken topic between them hangs in the air, suffocating them in the crawl spaces of the sixth floor. It was so heavy, it drove the two up, early.

Asin comes over, handing a pouch over to Daniel. He hefts the pouch, a part of him wondering if she's giving him more than his share before he shakes his head, clearing it. Liev is right; this was beginning to be a distraction.

While Daniel battles with his doubts, Asin has turned away and started off.

"Asin!" Daniel calls out.

Shoulders hunching slightly, the Catkin turns to look at Daniel, golden eyes glinting with expectation.

"We need to talk," Daniel says as he approaches her.

She chuffs, then nods finally, waving him ahead. Daniel rolls his eyes, wondering why he's always leading. For a time, Daniel debates where to go before defaulting to where he feels most comfortable – the Spinning Top.

***

The Top is surprisingly quiet, and Daniel blinks, surprised at the lack of patrons. Elise smiles as they come in, waving them over to a table and coming over to serve them herself. "Daniel, and this must be Asin?"

Asin nods and Elise smiles, "I know what he wants, but we have Burdock root if you wish? And the roast is just about ready."

Asin lets out a little yowl of delight, nodding to Elise's suggestions who smiles, moving off to get their order sorted. Daniel shifts uncomfortably in his chair as Asin turns to regard him, silent. They just sit there, waiting for the food to come, the silence growing increasingly uncomfortable before Daniel finally gives in.

"We're having problems," Daniel begins and waits for a reaction from Asin. Getting none, he forges on anyway, "We aren't working as well together, we're getting in each other's way, and well, it's just not going well."

Asin finally relents and offers him a short nod before Daniel continues, "It started with the fight with the Boss. And the healing. I guess, I guess you want to know why I didn't tell you about it before."

Asin tilts her head for a moment before letting out a little chuff and shakes it. "Stone."

"You are upset with me about the stone?" Daniel blinks, not exactly what he was thinking.

"Yes. I give. You refuse," Asin continues, shaking her head. "Throw away."

"Of course I refused it," Daniel states. "I can't take everything for myself. That would be wrong. You don't take from your team."

"Throw away!" Asin snarls and points. "No respect Asin."

"I do respect you. That's why I refused the stone!" Daniel protests and Asin huffs, nostrils flaring out as her tail swishes out behind her, straight as a sword.

"No respect. Throw away!" Asin snarls again and thumps her paw down, claws coming out slightly.

Daniel leans back away from the Catkin, the snarl sending involuntary shivers deep down his back, "Asin, I do respect you. You're my team."

Asin snarls again, but before she can speak, Elise appears carrying their drinks. "You two, calm down. Or do it outside of my inn."

Daniel blinks and notes how everyone is watching the two of them. He hangs his head slightly while Asin looks around, realises she's actually jumped up onto her chair as she speaks with Daniel and hops back down, looking slightly abashed as well. Elise, seeing the two have begun to behave themselves points her fingers at the two of them. "You two should actually try talking."

"We are!" Daniel exclaim and Elise reaches over, smacking him on the top of his head.

"I said talk, not shout the same things over and over again. Explain your side of things!" Shaking her head Elise walks out, muttering, "Youngsters," under her breath.

As Elise leaves the two of them, it is Asin who breaks the silence first, "Asin give gift. Gift! Daniel throw away. Throw away gift. Throw away respect." Finishing, Asin chuffs and reaches for her drink, guzzling it down.

Daniel frowns, shaking his head. "But I couldn't take it from you. You earned it!" At Asin's glare, he holds up a hand, trying to figure out how to explain. "You know I grew up in the mines, right?" Asin nods and Daniel continues, "The mines, you work in a team. Always. The stupid ones, the prospectors, the fools, they work alone and die alone. Real miners, we work together because the mine is always looking to end you. Cave-ins, monsters, bad pockets of air.

Without your team, you are nothing. *Without Asin, I would be nothing in the Dungeon.* And you never take all the ore, all the mana from another. If you do, they might not be able to come back the next day."

Asin snorts at the last bit, but chuffs a little, shaking her head. She's slightly mollified by what Daniel has said, but is still upset. As the two Adventurers ponder the matter, Elise arrives with their dinner, shooting them one last quelling look as business is finally picking up. Hurrying away, Elise leaves the two to sit in silence, enjoying the roast.

When dinner is finished, Asin fishes in her pocket and lays out a pair of silver. She looks Daniel straight in the eye and says, "Dinner. Gift."

Daniel nods at her words, murmuring a soft, "Thank you!" This was one battle he would not fight. Satisfied, Asin slinks off, the crowd of Adventurers and guards eyeing the Catkin and smiling as she leaves.

Chapter 23

"This is the Adventurer you mentioned?" The speaker is broad-shouldered with an erect bearing and a small, faded scar on his left cheek, wearing the green and gold uniform of the Army. The man speaks to Liev as he points a finger at Daniel who is enjoying his breakfast in the early morning.

Liev nods, hands folded behind his back, and surprisingly his unruly red hair combed flat, "Yes, Champion, he is. This is Daniel Chai, Healer and Adventurer."

Striding over, the Champion barks to Daniel in an authoritative voice that brooks no argument, "I have need of another Healer. Pay's a gold and a half a day for a Healer; we'll be gone for a week at most. We leave tomorrow."

His mouth full, Daniel chews and swallows quickly, casting a pitiful glance at Liev for a further explanation as he does so.

"This is Champion Eronin from the Duke's Guard. It seems that an Orc raiding party has been spotted two days' ride from here and the Champion has volunteered to fight it. You'll be joined by a dozen other Adventurers and a platoon of the Duke's Guard."

Quest Offered
Accompany Champion Eronin in battling the Orc Raiding Party.

Reward: 1 and a half gold a day as a Healer.

"Umm…" Daniel scratches at his chin as he finishes swallowing, "I'd be happy to do so, but I do work with another Adventurer, Asin. She uses knives, but she's a much better tracker than me."

"A gold a day," Eronin states and begins to turn around. He stops as Liev clears his throat, waiting for the Champion to turn to him. "Champion, I am afraid I must inform you, as per your request, that she is a Catkin."

"What?" Eronin turns and looks at his potential healer and then the Guild attendant. "Forget it. We don't need those thieving creatures in the group. Just you, Healer."

"Then no," Daniel states calmly, though the words make the entire room fall silent. Elise, having come out from the kitchen winces, matronly brown eyes narrowing in concern.

"Do you know who I am?" Eronin growls, leaning forwards to stare straight into Daniel's eyes. "You will come with me."

"No." Daniel meets the gaze for a brief moment and then is forced to look away, unable to meet the pressure exerted by the man's presence. Yet, stubborn nature refuses to give in to the man's demands. He would not abandon his team.

A hand slams into the table again, Eronin snarling, "I could destroy you for this insolence."

"Champion…" Liev intervenes, coughing into his hand. "As per Guild charter, an Adventurer may turn down any request, for any reason, so long as he has not previously accepted it. Daniel is within his rights, if not his mind."

Eronin snarls, a hand trembling on the table before he regains control of his temper and stalks out of the room, shoving the door open with a crash, Liev following silently behind. As they leave, Daniel feels a hard smack on the top of his head, Elise holding the offending spoon.

"You idiot! That was the Duke's Champion!" Elise complains, pointing towards the recently departed figure. "If you had played nice you could have gotten personal quests and more!"

Daniel rubs his head, trying to figure out how to explain this to Elise. She needed an explanation, probably one that was complicated, but it was simple really. Asin was his friend and his partner, and you always worked with your team because that's what you did in the mines. Once you had a partner, you worked together, no matter what. Eventually, he tries with, "I work with Asin."

Elise's groan is what he expected, though having overheard their previous conversation, she understands his thinking, to a point. Still, the damnable stubborn child! While she is standing there, frustrated, Daniel switches topics to something that puzzles him. "I didn't think Liev disliked her too."

Elise rubs her temples as she stares at Daniel, a headache forming while she explains to him, "Liev is just doing his job. The Champion doesn't work with Beastkin, and probably made that clear in his quest."

"Oh," Daniel frowns and looks at his hands, trying to understand the reasoning behind such a decision. In the end, he shrugs and dismisses it. It was not his concern why others chose to do what they did, just what he chose to do himself. Gulping down the last of his meal, Daniel stands and gives Elise a peck on the cheek. He and Asin were going to try fighting a single Ogre today on the seventh floor. Working the seventh floor was tough, and they had avoided the Titanic Crawler for the last few days as their close defeat was still fresh in their minds. Perhaps trying the new floor would provide much-needed variety, even if Daniel still didn't have the money for proper chain mail.

***

"This was not what I was expecting," Daniel mutters, staring around the seventh floor. The ceiling stretches for a good forty feet; glow stones are interspersed throughout the ceiling so that it looks like daylight itself in the cavern. The ground is covered in lush grass and occasional small trees, and more often bushes range across their view.

Asin nods firmly, gliding soundlessly across the grass in her light leather armour and boots before tentatively poking at a bush. When nothing happens, she squats down and eyes it closer, before shrugging and moving to the next type to repeat her actions.

Daniel keeps watch of the cavern while she does her thing, a part of him glad that he's no longer forced to crouch. If not for good massages, and a constant barrage of healing spells, he felt he would be stuck in a permanent half-crouch after the last several months.

A low rhythmic thudding brings both Adventurers' attention back to point, Asin pulling her cloak tighter before working her way into the shadows. Daniel steps forward to face the new threat and then gulps as he spots an Ogre for the first time, his hands growing clammy. Nine feet tall, wearing a ragged loincloth and wielding a club, the creature sports a potbelly and a pig-snout that is just the tip of a truly ugly but humanoid visage. It roars at seeing an intruder in its domain, rushing forwards to punish Daniel.

Daniel tenses, watching for the club to begin its strike as he forces himself to breathe slowly. The first battle was always the most dangerous as no knowledge of the monster's proclivities were available to draw upon. Rather than rushing in, Daniel intends to focus on defence instead. The club begins its downward swing, but Daniel does not move, instinct telling him to hold still until the Ogre is fully committed to the attack. The Ogre does not feint though, continuing the motion with ever-increasing speed so that Daniel has to throw himself aside, forced to give up an opportunity to counter to just dodge the blow. This is not like fighting the Crawlers or Kobolds; the fight reminds him more of training against Litzburn, a situation where his opponent had cunning and guile.

As the Ogre winds up to swing again, it is shocked by Asin's knife thrown from her hiding place. The knife pierces the Ogre's back, digging into its spine and stunning it for a moment. More knives land in quick succession and Daniel takes advantage of the momentary opening to slam his mace into the Ogre's knee twice before he springs back from the retaliatory attack. As the Ogre swings again, Daniel sheds the swing with his shield but is over-powered by the Ogre's strength and is driven to his knees. The Ogre continues to swing, each blow smashing aside Daniel's attempts at parrying, staggering the Adventurer beneath his shield. Each parried blow sends shudders of pain through his body, his shoulder and arms taking the abuse as his shield begins to crack.

As the Ogre steps forward again, Asin throws another Piercing Shot, this time aimed at its already injured knee. The knee gives way, and Daniel throws himself into a roll to avoid the falling monster. Asin continues to pelt the Ogre with her throwing knives, each knife sinking into its body with little resistance and shocking the creature with lightning, even as Daniel returns to beat on the Ogre with his mace. Crippled, the Ogre does not last much longer before succumbing to the attacks of the merciless Adventurers.

As the body fades, they find only a few coins left behind and a mana stone. The now experienced Adventurers immediately eye the stone, satisfied at the increase in quality once again before Asin tucks the stone away.

"You know, I felt kind of bad there..." Daniel says as he rubs his shoulder. The repeated attacks have numbed his arm and injured his left shoulder, the shield slightly cracked under the onslaught. His knee throbs as well from where he was forced to the ground. Nothing that a simple Minor Heal would not fix, which is what he does immediately, sighing in pleasure at the lack of pain.

Asin shrugs, not understanding Daniel's feelings on this. It was a monster. The Ogre needed to die, no matter how much it looked like a human or how helpless it was at the end. A Dungeon-created monster wasn't even real, not in the sense that sentient races were real. Just constructs.

Daniel looks out over the landscape before them before turning to Asin, "Up or stay?"

Asin ponders the question, thinking about the hallways above. The mana stone they had just received was definitely a level higher, which meant more copper. She hated being in debt, especially with her other obligations. More money faster was good, but it was dangerous too. Daniel had struggled to fight a single Ogre – what if two came? On the other hand, her daggers were much more effective against the Ogres with their current lack of armour.

Daniel is doing the maths in his own head as well, weighing the risk and reward of staying on the seventh floor. It seemed they could handle a single Ogre without injury. Two might be problematic, especially as Asin's knives were damaging but not deadly. He would have to focus almost exclusively on defence if he had to fight two. Still, he probably could do it…

"Stay." The two speak at almost the same time and then Asin chuffs in amusement. Decision made, she lopes ahead to check out potential problems, though a part of her resolves to avoid having to fight more than one at a time if it can be helped. Best to be careful.

***

"Elsa." Daniel smiles slightly, spotting the attendant in the Guild hall as the pair limp in, looking the worse for wear. The seventh floor had been tough, and thrice they had decided to stay hidden or bypass corridors rather than fight a pair of Ogres. However, the floor had been highly profitable in both experience and mana stones. He passes her the collected stones, watching her tally the stones. "Where's Liev?"

"Mmm…? Oh, he took the day off." Elsa smiles at him, her dirty blonde hair momentarily covering her eyes. She sweeps her hair aside, smiling up at the young Adventurer. He and his Catkin associate were the talk of the Guild, their progress the best the Guild had seen in the last few years. Why, they were down on the seventh floor already! Most Adventurers who chose to complete the Dungeon found themselves stuck on the sixth floor for at least a year, grinding levels till they could gain enough strength or a Skill Proficiency to destroy the Titanic Crawler.

"Really?" Daniel frowns, concern flashing across his face. Was the old bureaucrat sick?

"Mmm… most people don't work every day," Elsa says.

"Yeah, but…" Daniel doesn't know what to say to that, after all, Liev has been here every time he's been here.

Asin is chuffing beside him, obviously amused. Elsa just points a finger at her and says, "You're his partner. You're in here just as much as he is."

"Makes. Me."

Elsa just looks at the money crazy Catgirl, after all, Elsa was Asin's unofficial attendant. She was the one who Asin came to when she needed to find a partner who would work as hard as she did and who wouldn't hold her race against her. Asin pretends to miss the look, scratching at her own ear.

A gentle cough reminds Elsa that they still haven't been paid out yet, at which point she returns to her work, point having been made. Sometimes, these youngsters really didn't know when to stop.

Chapter 24

Days after the not so subtle hinting by Elsa, Daniel finds himself standing outside the Top, dressed comfortably in his only other pair of clean, non-adventuring clothing, waiting for Asin. He sighs, wishing for once she'd turn up on time for something other than a dungeon delve.

Just as he thinks that, he spots her and Khy'ra walking together, chatting amiably. As he gets over his surprise at Asin's apparent talkativeness, he gets another one as they close enough for him to hear the meows and growls that the two speak in. He didn't know Khy'ra spoke Catkin!

"Khy'ra!" He gives a quick peck to the offered cheek, sliding a hand around her waist and copping a quick feel. She rolls her eyes, but hugs him nonetheless, melding her body comfortably to his. "You didn't tell me you were coming."

"Asin came by the Clinic a few days ago to invite me." Khy'ra smiles and Asin nods in confirmation. Pointing down the street, the Catkin heads down, the mixed-race trio garnering more than a few quick stares. Daniel ignores it, focusing on his companions.

"Where are we going?" Daniel asks once again. Perhaps this time he'll get an actual answer.

"Celebration. Anika," Asin replies in her usual terse matter. Daniel rolls his eyes and is suddenly glad of Khy'ra's presence. He shoots an imploring look at Khy'ra who runs a hand through her hair, green eyes sparkling.

"It's the Beastkin celebration for Anika, their First Hero," Khy'ra says. "I believe today would mark the 497th anniversary of the founding of the city of Marloo by Anika, the first major step to the creation of Garhwa and thus the first Beastkin nation."

Daniel scratches his head and sighs, somewhat abashed at his lack of knowledge. Spending most of his time in the mines, dominated by humans and the occasional dwarf, he had little knowledge of the other races. It just had never been part of his world view till now.

Asin does not lead them straight to the Beastkin district though, instead stopping by a butcher's first. Unlike many, the butcher seems more than happy to see Asin, as Asin is one of her most regular and best customers. Today's order was noteworthy, even for the small carnivore, and Asin quickly drags Daniel over to help with the large sack.

"This thing must weigh a good eighty pounds! What did you do? Buy a whole pig?" Daniel grumbles as he lifts the sack. Asin's cheerful nod makes him groan again, but he stays silent as they continue the walk, Khy'ra regretfully detached from Daniel's arm now.

They continue to journey through the streets of Karlak, Khy'ra, as always, smiling and nodding to those she recognises. The elf, as usual, garners more than one admiring glance, though most either dismiss Asin's presence or watch her extra carefully. After a time, the trio leave the normal thoroughfares that Daniel knows, the roads becoming narrower, buildings growing older and more rundown, though still well washed and well kept. The transition is gradual at first, but as they step out from another alleyway, it's like walking into another city.

The streets are filled with Beastkin of all kinds, from arrogant Wolfkin to the statelier Catkin, grumbly Jackals, lazy Ursines and more. As great a surprise for Daniel, however, are the riot of colours and smells that make up the streets. A wild divergence from humanity's boring pastels are the vibrant colours that the Beastkin coat their dwellings in, yellows and greens and reds cover walls and wood trim and are even layered on roofs. For the celebration, strings of red and white flow from one side of the alley to the other, with trailing hand-painted scrolls depicting memorable scenes beneath. Food and other scents cling to the air, mixing with wild abandon and assaulting Daniel's senses and he reels, wondering how the Beastkin are able to handle all this. Even his human senses are over-whelmed, how do they cope?

By his side, both Asin and Khy'ra watch with amusement, treasuring the view as Daniel struggles to deal with the overload. When he finally recovers, Asin tugs on his hand and points, leading him to a cooking pit that has been set up in front of a shop where he is directed to set the pig.

A rumbly, growly conversation ensues between Asin and the presiding cook, both getting more and more agitated. Daniel frowns, hairs prickling on the back of his neck and he unconsciously reaches for his non-existent mace. Khy'ra reaches for and grabs his hand, pulling him close to whisper, "It's okay, they're just arguing about how to cook the meat. Beastkin are loud amongst themselves."

Daniel grimaces and sighs, watching his normally quiet companion get into a shouting match. Unsure what to do, the two lovers stand and watch the scenes around them, ignoring the arguing pair; Beastkin children stream through the streets in a never-ending game of tag, miraculously dodging busy adults without fail. A large, black Catkin dressed in a garishly coloured yellow tunic and blousy white pants strides up to the pair, hands splayed with paws facing the sky in greeting. He is a mixture of human and Catkin traits, a feline-angled face but lacking the over-abundance of fur that marks Asin's own visage. "Khy'ra and Daniel, it must be. May you find safety at our fires."

Khy'ra copies the hand greeting, and after a brief moment so does Daniel. She intones the ritual response as well, "Elder Chetan, may your fire burn forever safely."

Unsure if he should repeat the message, Daniel just falls back on being silent. Elder Chetan turns to the young Adventurer, black fur wrinkling in amusement before he speaks, only the slightest of growls marring his voice, "Thank you for coming. And thank you for taking care of my daughter."

"Daughter…" Daniel catches on quickly enough and shakes his head. "We take care of each other. We're partners."

The Elder chuffs and continues, "Yes. It is good that she has found one who is willing to accept her. Asin has not had it easy, being closer to the progenitor than many other Kin."

Daniel's puzzled look encourages the Elder to explain further, first stepping closer to allow himself to lower his voice, "It is strange. In Garhwa, she would be exalted. Here, in Brad, we strive to be closer to you humans, and she is despised." Ears drooping, the Elder shrugs. "I love my daughter, but she could have made it easier on herself too. She is stubborn and prideful, much like her mother."

Daniel smiles slightly, having noticed both aspects of his companion on more than one occasion. She could be frustrating at times to deal with, but so could he, he had been told.

"Still, this is not the time for this! Come, you must drink some saboo and dance!" The Elder claps his paws together and drags the two off, growling out his intentions to his daughter who just waves him away. The argument with that obstinate cook who wishes to use wyxli spice on her pig had to be completed. *Wyxli spice! Everyone knew you used jylin leaves and cracked esper spice to get the best taste from roast pig.*

The ensuing hours pass in laughter and amusement, the Elder happy to play host to the two guests. As the day progresses, Daniel notes that his and Khy'ra's presence is a notable exception, the Beastkin having the run of this neighbourhood to themselves. That is other than a loud and boisterous Tharuk, partaking in a drinking competition with a bear which neither seems ready to concede. Through the day, Daniel has food and drink stuffed into his hands continuously, meats of various types such that even his own carnivorous nature is more than fulfilled.

Only once is there silence, when the sun reaches its zenith. The Beastkin pause, staring at the sky, the silence lingering for minutes. At first, the growls are too low for Daniel to hear, though he can feel it in his bones as the voices of the assembled Beastkin surround him. Slowly, it goes higher and higher, the growls resolving into an animalistic song that tugs at a deeply hidden part of him. When the song is over, Daniel finds himself breathing heavily as if from a long run, his face flushed and his eyes sparkling. A glance at Khy'ra shows that even the Elven beauty is affected, the smouldering look she gives him makes him wonder briefly if he can find an empty room somewhere.

Asin joins them soon after the ceremony and drags Daniel to a nearby warehouse where a small arena has been created. There, Beastkin challenge each other in various feats of athleticism. Once, even Daniel is dragged into the centre to join in the feat of strength, though he is quickly outclassed by the massive Ursine and Buffalo

Beastkin who make up the majority of the contestants. It is Khy'ra who proves the surprise, laughingly dancing and stealing ribbons in the game of tag and agility that the Catkin and Snakes dominate otherwise. Eventually, even she is caught but many of the Beastkin eye the Elf with new respect.

During a lull in the evening, Daniel finally manages to ask the question that has disturbed him all day, "Asin's very talkative, isn't she."

"Yes, yes she is," Khy'ra answers.

"So, why doesn't she talk to me?" Daniel grumbles.

"Do you talk to her in Beastkin?"

"No…" Daniel frowns. "She seems to understand me well…"

"Yes, dear," Khy'ra sighs and touches his throat and then hers. "Now look at hers."

Daniel does as she says, finally looking and then slowly blinks, feeling ashamed, "She has trouble speaking doesn't she?"

"In Brad? Yes."

Daniel falls silent then, absently chewing on the rib he is given. He stops, grimacing and puts the food down again as his stomach catches up to his hands. Way too much food. Khy'ra pushes his shoulder with her own, and he meets her eyes, where she just shakes her head slightly. Getting the message, he focuses on having fun. This is not the time for such thoughts. Smiling, he holds a hand out and Khy'ra takes it, letting herself be pulled onto the dance floor again with a laugh.

Chapter 25

"There you are!" Liev's sudden appearance makes the two Adventurers jump, Asin making it half-way up the nearest wall while Daniel drops into a crouch, shield up. They then both blink, after all, they're both on the seventh floor working their way through a couple of Ogres and Liev had never been spotted anywhere close to the Dungeon before. "Take my hand."

Daniel frowns and Liev sighs, no longer asking and reaching out to grab his hand and Asin's arm in short order. A surge of power takes them both out of the Dungeon directly into a room that neither has seen before. The two Adventurers stare around themselves dumbfounded, a window to the outside room indicating that they are in town and in the Guild itself.

"How…?" Daniel says.

"Group Teleport. It's a level 50 Adventurer's Skill Proficiency," Liev explains as he gestures to Daniel. 'Come, you're needed."

Daniel automatically follows but then stops short, Liev is pointing to Asin who has started to come too. "Your presence will be unhelpful, my dear. We go to see the Champion. And don't give me that look, Daniel, we need your Gift."

Daniel wipes the mulish look off his face, grimacing and following after the fast disappearing attendant. He frowns in thought though, surprised to find that Liev was, or perhaps still is, a high-level Adventurer. Liev certainly didn't have the bearing of a fighter. In fact, the thought of Liev holding a sword makes Daniel chuckle to himself internally, the bookish and fastidious red-haired older gentleman ignorant of Daniel's amusement.

"The Champion and his party were ambushed. Most died in the attack, and the Champion himself is gravely injured. We need you to heal him, Daniel," Liev says.

"Uhh…" Daniel's initial amusement is wiped away at Liev's words as he struggles to catch up mentally.

Liev turns, getting into Daniel's face and speaking emphatically, "Young man, I understand your position. I almost admire it. However, this is not the time or place. The Orcs haven't sent a raiding party; they sent a War Party. There are over three hundred Orcs rampaging through the province at this moment and that man, for all of his distasteful views, is the most powerful weapon we have. If. He. Survives."

Daniel gulps, the thought of three hundred Orcs laying waste to the countryside enough to force him to cast aside any personal feelings he had. While he was no Healer, he understood their oath – to treat all that needed it, no matter their personal feelings. Daniel nods firmly, and in silence the pair hurry to the barracks where the Champion lies injured.

The sight that greets Daniel when he enters makes him pale. The Champion, once a larger than life presence is gravely hurt, multiple open wounds on his chest and limbs. Most dangerous of all was the distorted skull - pressure and shattered bones causing it to bulge out. For a moment, Daniel can only stare before he takes a deep shuddering breath.

A hand touches Daniel's, gripping tight and he notices for the first time the presence of others in the room. The Guard Captain he knows by sight, Khy'ra obviously, but the other three are unknown to him. The first seems to be another healer from the way he works on the Champion's wounds but who the other two are he is unable to guess. One is a portly human with a beard, the other a female with a thick gold chain around her neck. The chain clues him in on her at last – that was the Merchant Guild's seal on it. Khy'ra squeezes his hand again, bringing his attention back to her.

"Can you heal him?"

Daniel nods mutely, a part of him already assessing the damage and what he would need to do. The greater part of his mind though stalls at the cost of the healing, a cost that would dwarf anything he had done in years. Only once before had he attempted something this powerful, and in that case, he had eventually failed. No Gift could win against the ravages of time, not in the end.

"Daniel," Khy'ra turns her lover's gaze to meet hers, concern etching her voice. "What's wrong?"

"My Gift..." he struggles against his irrational fear of telling them, the fear that they will exploit him, what they will ask of him, force on him. His hand, entwined with hers begins shaking violently.

"What is the holdup?" the portly human speaks imperiously, pointing. "Heal him, Adventurer. I won't have the Baron's Champion die in my city!"

Khy'ra turns to the man, shooting a glare that would have killed if it could. Liev steps in, holding a hand up, "My Lord Mayor, this space is no longer suitable for non-Healers. I believe we should retire."

"I'm the Mayor!" Snapping, the portly man begins to set himself when the woman leans over, whispering in his ear. He grunts and finally stomps out, followed closely by the woman and Liev. Just before she leaves, she casts an assessing glance at the pale Daniel before turning away. The Healer, after a glance at Khy'ra, moves to a corner, giving the two space.

"Daniel, talk to me. Please…" Khy'ra implores him, holding both their hands up and placing a kiss on the top of his.

Daniel draws a deep shuddering breath and then whispers, softly, "When I use my Gift, I lose a bit of myself. A part of what I've learnt, a part of my memories, a part of my skills and some of my energy. The Gift, it strips me of these things when I use it. It's normally not much, just a few minutes here or there, an hour or two sometimes. This though…" He shivers again, clutching her hand, "I could lose a lot more."

Khy'ra's eyes widen, remembering all the times she blithely asked him to help her in the

Clinic, all the times he seemed a bit forgetful or slow afterwards. All the times he acceded without protest when he should have said no, "You… you… idiot!"

"Yeah." His secret out, he seems to relax a bit. "This has to happen, doesn't it?"

Lips pursed, Khy'ra nods, "It does. The Champion's another Gifted. If he is able to use his Gift, only a Master Mage or another Gifted can challenge him on the field of battle."

Daniel lets her hands go, and walks past her to put his hands on the struggling Champion. Almost plaintively, as he thrusts his Gift into the man, he says, "Couldn't he at least be a little nicer?"

Khy'ra watches for a moment as Daniel begins, then turns, gesturing for the other Healer to keep an eye on them. She has another place to be; there are words to be spoken. If what Daniel fears is true, he will lose much in this, and she intends to ensure he is well compensated for it.

Focused, Daniel misses the byplay. His Gift tells him all the details he needs, the punctured lung, the shredded intestines, the broken skull and the ever-growing pressure in the head, barely relieved by other methods. A normal human being would have been dead a score over, only the Champion's stupendous health and the magic used on him are managing to keep him alive. Yet his health falls with each breath; he will not last long without further healing.

Damage assessed, Daniel begins the process of fixing things. Plugging the most dangerous wounds first, he heals and lowers the pressure in the Champion's skull while bones shift back under the skin to their appropriate locations. Each pulse of power pulls another memory, another shudder through his body as his Gift strips him of recently learnt skills, of muscle and real memory. It is an uncaring taskmaster, removing both pleasant and unpleasant memories, caring not of their origin. The Champion's health works against Daniel now, muscles and organs that would be pliant and easy to heal in another being requiring more energy, more time, more experience than any previous patient.

What feels like hours, but is barely half of one, passes by before Daniel pulls his senses back into himself. He stumbles, collapsing into a thoughtfully positioned chair as the Champion's breath eases. The Champion's wounds are mostly healed, the majority fixed and he no longer does injury to himself with every breath. Bruises and some cuts still lie across the Champion's body, but Daniel knows he is no longer in danger. Regular magical healing or plain time will do the rest.

Level Lost!
You are now a Level 4 Adventurer
Attribute Points Lost

That could have been worse... Daniel stares at the little sliver of Experience he has left keeping him from falling another level and groans. So much

190

experience; so much time lost. Months of hard work, stripped from him, his memory of recent Dungeon delves and fights gone. His body aches from the use of the Gift, his nerves and muscles feel stripped raw. However, the job is not done, and so he forces himself upright, placing his hand on the Champion's chest and invoking his healing spell. He was so close to getting the option to learn a Moderate Heal the next time he received proficiency, so close to becoming more than he was before. Once more, he has been dragged down by his Gift, and he can't help but feel a flare of resentment. He forces it down, focusing on burning through his Mana to finish the job. Later. Later he'll deal with this.

With the last of his mana drained from him, Daniel turns away to leave. They can deal with the rest of this. All he wants is rest. As he steps aside, an iron grip grasps his arm.

"You healed me," the Champion rumbles, awake.

"Yes," Daniel says, tugging at his arm. The Champion releases him and stares at the youngster who dared defy him days ago.

"Why?"

"It was needed," Daniel begins and falls silent.

"And the Cost?" Daniel hears the capitalization; he understands what the Champion asks. Another one cursed/blessed with a Gift at birth understands all too well the Cost incurred. It was no simple matter, no matter what the others thought. The Champion's own Gift allowed him to ignore any attack he chose to when invoked, but the price was paid in pain days later. The longer the Gift was activated, the worst and longer the pain it inflicted. The payment could be put-off, but not indefinitely.

Daniel shakes his head, refusing to answer. He owes this man no answer. He owes him nothing more. Duty done, all Daniel wants is to be left alone now, and so he tugs again at the arm, the Champion finally releasing him. Daniel walks away, leaving the Champion to the care of the Guards' Healer. Behind him, the Champion growls, displeased at being so casually dismissed once again. *Damn the child!*

***

In another room, while Daniel works, a larger and more intense argument is happening. In that room, the Mayor and the Merchant Guild Master and Khy'ra face-off over what Daniel's fee for the healing will be. Liev watches, taking no side in the argument directly, though he subtly helps by pointing out the rarity and exclusivity of Daniel's Gift.

It is only when the Guards' Healer arrives to announce the successful restoration of the Champion that the argument finishes. Like all good negotiations, no single party leaves happy, but Khy'ra is grimly content at least. If the child would not value himself, then she would ensure that.

Back in the Top, in his room, alone, Daniel calls up his Status Screen to see how much he has lost in detail.

Name: Daniel Chai
Class: Level 4 Adventurer (2%)
Sub-classes: Level 7 (Miner) (14%)
Human (Male)

Statistics
Life: 201
Stamina: 201
Mana: 152

Attributes
Strength: 18
Agility: 19
Constitution: 26
Intelligence: 16
Willpower: 18
Luck: 13

Skills
Unarmed Combat: Level 3 (01/100)
Clubs: Level 8 (14/100)
Shield: Level 6 (28/100)
Dodge: Level 4 (36/100)
Combat Sense: Level 5 (48/100)
Perception: Level 5 (36/100)
Mining: Level 7 (78/100)
Healing: Level 8 (17/100)
Herb Lore: Level 3 (31/100)
Stealth: Level 2 (14/100)

Cooking: Level 2 (37/100)
Singing: Level 2 (14/100)

Skill Proficiencies
Double Strike
Shield Bash
Mapping (II)

Spells
Minor Healing (I)

Gifts
Martyr's Touch - The caster may heal oneself or others by touch and concentration, sacrificing a portion of his life to do so. Cost varies depending on the extent of the injuries healed.

Chapter 26

"Asin, we have to do the fifth floor today," Daniel announces to his friend the next day. She stops from touching the gem that would bring them lower, tilting her head as she considers Daniel. He did seem weaker today – perhaps his healing had drained him more than she thought. She chuffs out, slightly annoyed but touches the fifth-floor gemstone.

Relieved that she will not enquire further, Daniel follows his friend down. It's time to see how much he has lost. Three nests later, Daniel takes out his frustration on a single Crawler that they have come across, slamming down again and again with his mace. So much lost. He's a step slower, a beat off and while he feels he should be faster, he's not, and he knows why.

Behind him, Asin watches with deep concern. Daniel's normal calm, slightly amused but entirely engaged mode of adventuring is gone, replaced with a short, sullen ball of fury and resentment. On the other hand, as Daniel kicks the Crawler away and moves on to the next cavern, he certainly is making up for the quality with quantity today. Grabbing the mana stone, Asin moves to keep up with her friend and to ensure he doesn't walk into any traps. Well, if Daniel keeps this up too long, she'll find a barrel of water and dump him in it. Till then, she is content to let him work his feelings out on the Crawlers.

In a room far above the Dungeon, the titular leaders of the city of Karlak work out plans to deal with the rampaging War Party.

***

"Daniel, a word?" Liev is waiting for them when they finally surface from the Dungeon. Daniel nods, moving to the side to allow to Asin handle the sale of their mana stones and other loot.

"Firstly, thank you." Liev does not stop though, knowing the young Adventurer was uncomfortable with thanks, "Secondly, there has been a general request for Adventurers to join the army as ancillary troops due to the War Party. I have taken the liberty of assigning you and Asin to Maximillian's team as melee fighters. I believe that is where your particular skills will be most useful."

Daniel frowns and Liev sighs, explaining, "Doing so ensures you are not conscripted as a Healer if the number of volunteers is deemed insufficient. In addition, it will be good experience for you, young man. Brad does not have to keep a large standing army because it relies on its Adventurers to provide additional troops when necessary. If you intend to progress as an Adventurer, you will find that such requests become more and more common. This particular event is as safe as any general Army sponsored-quest will be."

"Yes, sir," Daniel finally agrees. He is still not certain joining the army was a great option for him, but if Liev felt it was the right thing to do, he would accede to the man's request. The attendant had yet to steer him wrong.

"Lastly, you are going to be very popular among your peers in short order. Word of your Gift has finally reached their ears after yesterday's incident." Liev hesitates and falls silent, leaving any additional advice unspoken. Truthfully, Liev had done as much as he could. Getting the young man out of town under the watchful eye of a friend ensured that those who would use him just for his Gift had no target, at least for the short term. In the meantime, he and Khy'ra would work on making his return as uncomplicated as possible.

Seeing no other conversational threads cropping up, Daniel wishes Liev goodbye and returns to Asin. He quickly informs her of their new quest to which she replies, "Pay?"

Daniel pauses, realising he never did ask that. Asin lets out an annoyed chuff, slinking back to talk with Liev directly, grumbling all the while about how lucky Daniel was that he was such a good distraction for her. Finding a comfortable corner, Daniel settles down to wait, knowing Asin will more than handle matters for both of them. He had spent the day fighting, going from one nest to the next and now he was drained, all his anger and regret smashed apart like the Crawlers he had met. When Asin is done, and has provided him with the details of their pay, he thanks her, and they part ways, Asin to spend an evening with family and Daniel to the Top.

At the Top, Daniel is startled to see Khy'ra waiting for him, chatting amiably with Elise. Khy'ra sends a smile his way, walking over to kiss him before wrinkling her nose at his smell.

"I was thinking dinner, but I think a bath would be better," Khy'ra says and points upwards. "Hurry up; I'll be waiting."

Daniel nods dumbly, deciding that it is best to go with the flow here. He did need a bath after all, or at least a wash. A quick trip upstairs to get a bar of soap and a change of clothing is all that is needed before he returns, Khy'ra taking his arm as they bid farewell.

The walk to the bathing room is short and pleasant, the two quickly catching each other up on their day's activities.

"…now Leon comes in with this barb in his foot, about two inches sticking right out of it. And he's sitting there, dripping blood in the waiting room and every time we go to get him in, he sends another patient in!" Khy'ra continues, shaking her head. "I eventually had to do the damn operation right there in the room and push it out in front of everyone. That big baby was so scared of it coming out that he nearly died of blood loss!"

Daniel laughs at her words, holding the door open for Khy'ra as they enter the bathtub. Both experienced hands, they deposit a silver coin each for their personal use and then Khy'ra deposits another three silver to get them a private room. When Daniel moves to protest, he is quelled by the smouldering look Khy'ra offers him.

A silly grin crosses his face as they head in, first to their respective sexes changing rooms before they make their way to the marked private room. Daniel is surprised to find Khy'ra in first, lounging in the circular wooden bath that is large enough to fit four in it. Steam comes from the hot water, a pair of small ladles and even soap set aside for their use. As he nears the tub, he realises that she is naked under the water.

"Mmm… I hadn't brought a change of clothing," she says in answer to his look.

Daniel grins, sliding in with her. Before he can move to get a kiss, she points to the soap, and he sighs, getting to scrubbing. As he moves to clean his back, she moves over and takes it up, scrubbing at his back.

"Liev tells me that you'll be joining the Army tomorrow," Khy'ra says.

"Yeah, he said it's good for me. I never really considered it, you know," Daniel says.

"Liev is somewhat traditional in his thinking. Not all Adventurers take as much part in the Army quests as he did, or thinks most should do. I rarely did," Khy'ra says, smiling and splashing his back before pushing back.

Daniel turns around, ducking under the water to get the last of the soap out of his eyes before he lies back, enjoying the heat as it releases his muscles, "Oh! That's nice…"

Smiling as she watches him, Khy'ra sighs and swims over, sliding between his legs and straddling him. When his eyes open, she puts a finger to his lips and murmurs, "Daniel, focus. I wanted to tell you something. You need to be careful about the quests you take. Most are, well, normal, but some might not sit well with you. Army quests aren't like your normal quests – you can't take one and then leave it just because you don't like how it works out or the information wasn't complete. You have to finish Army quests or face their censure."

Daniel pauses, staring into her eyes and then nods slowly, "Okay. I'll be careful."

Khy'ra smiles and then kisses him before murmuring. "Good, now we've got this room for another hour. Let's make the most of it."

***

The next morning, Asin and Daniel exit to meet up with the Army in the clear fields north of Karlak. Already, the first few divisions have gathered, their supply train pulling in behind them. In contrast to the orderly line-up of the army divisions, the Adventurers mill around in loose groups, individuals occasionally breaking off to chat with other groups.

The two friends glance around, feeling somewhat out of place. There are few Beastkin in the group, clustered together in small clumps. For the first time, Daniel realises how little interaction he has had with the general Adventuring population of the town of Karlak. Even the regulars he sees at the Top often receive little more than a nod. His own free time was mostly taken up by Khy'ra, the Clinic or training with the occasional night drinking with the Guards thrown-in. Unlike most Adventurers, his social circle was the town residents.

As the two stand around awkwardly, a tall, blond swordsman walks up to them clad in plate mail. He smiles as he nears, showing off perfect teeth on top of a chiselled jaw and Daniel feels a sudden twinge of jealousy. "Daniel? Asin?"

Receiving confirmation from both, the swordsman offers his hand, "Maximillian. You'll be in my party for this."

Daniel shakes it, impressed by the casual strength he feels through the handshake. Obviously, all those muscles were not just for show. Asin chuffs a greeting as well, eyeing the surroundings with casual interest.

"Come on; I'll introduce you to the rest of the group." Maximillian leads them through the crowd, offering quick nods and greetings as he walks through, the man's presence obviously well known. It takes them a short while to wind their way to their own party as there are nearly a hundred Adventurers gathered already. Daniel feels somewhat impressed, never realising there were this many in the town. Most are out-fitted like he is with varying degrees of protection for armour and weaponry, the vast majority being melee fighters. Only a small portion seem to be carrying a visible ranged weapon, and of those, crossbows seem to be the most popular option.

"Daniel, Asin, this is Kilroy and Mia. Mia's a Ranger and is our main ranged weapon dealer.

Kilroy's, well, Kilroy's Kilroy," Maxmillian says. "Have you shot a crossbow before Daniel?"

Daniel shakes his head, glancing at the weapon that Max holds out to him.

"No problem. We'll head down the way and get you familiar with it. It's simple compared to the bow, so you should pick it up easily. We'll all be using a ranged weapon, other than Asin for obvious reasons, and the crossbows and Mia's bow will be our first line of offence."

Daniel nods, hefting the crossbow and following along. He voices one hesitation first though, "Don't we have to join up the army?"

"There's no need right now. It'll take them forever to get moving, and we'll catch up once we're done training," Maximillian says, gesturing for them to catch up.

***

Daniel repeats quietly in his head the instructions he's been given - exhale, remember to adjust for the wind and drop, pull gently on the trigger – and feels the jerk as the crossbow bolt releases, flying to the target. Breath held, he watches the arrow arc through the air and miss once again, this time by 5 meters.

"I think you're getting worse," Maximillian says with awe.

"Worse," chuffs Asin before going back to cleaning her paw.

"I'm sorry," Daniel sighs, dejected. He reaches for another bolt and realises he's shot them all. A glance to the side shows that the others are done, for now, so he calls out his intention of retrieving the bolts, hurrying to do so. Four hours of training and he hasn't managed to hit the stump a bare 20 meters away even once.

When he returns, Maximillian shakes his head as Daniel begins to load the crossbow. "No time, we need to get going. We'll have you carry the crossbow and reload for Killroy instead."

Daniel looks away, shame filling him. A hand claps on his shoulder, Maximillian waiting for Daniel to look up before speaking, "It's okay. Not everyone can be good at everything. Now come on, we've got a bit of a hike before we're caught up."

Chapter 27

"Is this all they do?" grumbles Daniel, slogging along behind the army. He'd enjoy the countryside, but since the Adventurers were stuck behind both the army and the supply train, most of what he got to see was dust clouds and the turds he had to walk around.

"Pretty much," Maximillian chuckles, seemingly completely at ease even after a day and night of this. "Joining up with the army is mostly a lot of boredom, punctuated by a few hours or minutes of excitement."

"At least they get experience out of this," Daniel grumbles, waving his hand forward. Unlike Adventurers who mostly gained experience from exploring, killing and questing; the army gained theirs from training and marching for the most part. It was, in the opinion of many learned scholars, certainly better for professional armies to gain experience by training for war rather than actually waging war. Musing on this, Daniel is struck by a thought, "Max, how do Orcs gain experience?"

"Ah, you don't know?" Maximillian asks rhetorically. As more than one rookie Adventurer moves in, Max raises his voice, "Orcs are kind of like us – they gain experience mostly from killing and questing. However, unlike us and like the army, those in positions of power also gain a steady boost of experience. It's why your average Orc grunt is easy enough to fight, but their bosses are much more difficult."

"How much more?" Daniel asks.

"An Orc Boss is about twice as dangerous as you'd expect based on its level. Stronger, faster and smarter. Don't fight them if you can, that's what the Army Sergeants and the Advanced Adventurers are for," Maximillian responds, making sure to look at the rookies. There are more than a few nods including from Daniel and Asin. Daniel especially agrees, feeling particularly vulnerable after his recent loss of level.

***

At night, the campfires spread out over the plain. Each Adventuring group has created their own little camp, each scattered haphazardly, unlike the army. On cooking duty today, Daniel stirs the pot, ignoring the occasional proffered recommendation from Asin. Rumours swirl around them, that the Orcs were sighted earlier today, that they have left, that they destroyed one, two, no eleven villages already. After an exhausting first night listening to Rumours, Daniel resolves to ignore them all, focusing on what he can control - the stew.

It was strange, being out in the city, travelling to do battle with sentient creatures he had never seen before. He knew of the Orcs from rumours and late night tales, after all, their lands bordered Brad in the West, and they conducted regular raids into nearby villages on a regular basis. Yet, his upbringing in the mountains meant he had

had no direct interaction with them. Unlike humans, it seemed most of their levelling options required constant battle, forcing them into constant raids and attacks against each other and Brad itself. More than once, Brad had launched campaigns into Orc lands to destroy settlements and reduce the population, but the sprawling, untouched lands that the Orcs claimed meant that eventually the army campaign was called back and the Orcs would return. Rumours had it that Orcs gave birth in litters, their constant attacks and seemingly unending numbers resulting from their animalistic breeding patterns, unlike the more civilized and sentient races.

Daniel stirs the pot once more, tasting the stew before waving over his party members. It felt strange, to be grouped with so many others when it was just Asin and him for the longest time. Strange, but nice, even if this was temporary. His new party members were all good people, Kilroy, a joker; Maximillian, stern but kind; and Mia, quiet and competent. The quiet (and not so quiet when Kilroy was around) camaraderie was soothing, even as they all felt the tension of the upcoming battle.

Perhaps it was because they all risked their lives on a daily basis in the Dungeon that the Adventurers seemed to take it in their stride. Certainly, they were louder and more exuberant than their Army counterparts. More than once, he had caught the glowers from passing army personnel, almost as if they were angry that the Adventurers were willing to laugh. Yet, Daniel mused, what else could they do? Risking life for money was their way of life, and whether it was a Crawler which had dropped from the ceiling or an Orc who smashed their skulls in, it didn't matter how their lives ended. If you could not learn to laugh at upcoming death, you had no place being an Adventurer.

As Daniel sips on the stew and accepts praise for his cooking from all his party members but Asin, his thoughts turn to motivations. It was strange, how those in the Army, the Guard and Adventurers were so similar but so different. Each led a life of violence when a more peaceful life was an option, yet the individual motivations for each group were different - patriotism, service or adventure. Each gained strength in different ways too, training, peace or conflict and would eventually gain skills from their classes that marked them differently too. The Adventurers' inventory ability, the Guards' Truth Tell or the Brad Infantry's Shield Wall were all individual skill proficiencies that were available only to those who dedicated themselves to the lifestyle. Perhaps it was the class skills, the distinction those created that motivated an individual to go one way or the other – or perhaps it was the way experience was garnered. Certainly, the Guards in his experience were steadier, more prone to finding peaceful solutions than your average Adventurer.

It was a life that was far different from his time as a miner. Sometimes, he wondered if the others who chose a more peaceful, less dangerous life were correct – but like many of his peers, none of the other choices had felt right. No resource gathering, farming or crafting job would ever give him the chance to test himself like an Adventurer did. No guardsmen or soldier would ever have the freedom his vocation had.

Perhaps that's why he felt so much more at home among these Adventurers now than he ever had while mining, as the choices each of them had made separated them all from common society. Though, did perhaps the thrill fade away? Certainly, it seemed that old Adventurers stopped being Adventurers if Khy'ra, Liev and Tharuk were anything to go by. Perhaps Adventuring was a young man's job.

Daniel smiles slightly, accepting the bottle of spirit from Kilroy and pushes aside those thoughts as he joins them for a game of cards. Musings like this were interesting, but in the end, it made no real difference. He was an Adventurer now and soon they would fight.

***

"Well, I guess the easy money is over," Maximillian chuckles, eyeing the increased activity among the army personnel ahead of them. The army has been moving ahead on the road, heading closer and closer to the border with each mile across the rolling grassy plains. Perfect land for farming, with fertile soil and plentiful rainfall, if you discounted the constant slopes.

"Hmm…?" Daniel turns away from the exaggerated story told by Kilroy – there was no way three goats and a wolf did that with a farmer – when Maximillian speaks. He brushes a hand through his brown hair in absent thought, peering at the movement in the distance.

"Trouble looks like. If I'm correct, we'll get a message soon, and the wagons will be pulling to the side," Maximillian says, gesturing for them to hurry up a bit to stand next to their assigned wagon. Events fall true to his word, as word is soon sent back for the supply wagons to pull over and set-up for a potential attack in a small glen. The moment the wagons do so, the Adventuring groups spread out to stand guard while the wagon drivers and their attendants hurry to pull out any equipment needed. Ahead, the army pulls away from the road to the top of the hill, spreading out with the infantry in front and archers behind. At the top of the hill, the commanders and the Champion take their place, watching.

Daniel shifts from foot-to-foot, wanting a better view. Wanting to actually see the Orcs, but their job was simple – guard the supply train. Other Adventuring groups pull away, forming a smaller but more mobile force awaiting instructions, situated just behind the hill and to the right of the army. *Those lucky Adventurers would see actual battle*, thinks Daniel. That force would be used to help flank or reinforce the army as needed, a secondary reserve to the Army's own.

A hand drops on Daniel's shoulder, causing him to stop moving. Maximillian smiles, pointing to Daniel's back and speaking, "Might want to check that over. Don't load it yet though, we'll get a signal when things are about to start, but there's no reason not to check it now."

Daniel nods gratefully, falling to the task of checking the crossbow he carries as requested. Maximillian smiles, noting how the youngster calms down a little with something active to do. Of course, as Maximillian glances up to Daniel's original partner and thinks, some people could afford to be a bit more excited. Asin sees the glance and guesses Max's thoughts but just yawns, sharp teeth flashing in the sun as she stretches on top of the wagon they are guarding before lying back down.

Next to the nervous Daniel, Kilroy sets up with his crossbow, sticking a few bolts in the ground as does Mia. She strings her bow swiftly and with ease, testing the pull before going through a series of eye-catching, slow stretches. All around them, various other Adventurers take part in their preparation rituals, getting ready for the battle.

Time stretches on with no battle though, ticking by an hour after hour. No fight, no battle, and no sound from across the hill. The Adventurers get impatient, annoyed and then finally bored. They relax, sitting around and one group even starts a card game.

When the drums sound, everyone perks up again. Noise that was at first ignored brings everyone's attention back to where they are, the danger they are all in. Adventurers stand, and even the army that had been resting for a time straighten. The drums begin to grow in volume, accompanied by shouts and growls that travel across the hill. The roars grow louder, bugle calls of the Army finally sounding. Archers in the back row pull back and fire, sending arcs of arrows above the heads of their comrades, blows falling unseen by Daniel and the other Adventurers.

When the clash finally comes, the meaty smack of blood and bone against steel and wood, it resounds through the glen, amplified between the two hills. Screams begin soon after, cries of rage and pain intersperse between the all too regular sound of metal against metal and metal against flesh. The battle happens on the other side of the hill, for the most part, only the work of archers shooting over the hill seen, yet Daniel can imagine it.

Soon enough, the Adventurers grouped to the right are sent around the flank at a run as the Champion strides away from the command group, disappearing behind the hill in a straight line. Others from the command tent break away at intervals to meet greater threats in the Orc army directly. All this Maximillian explains to the novice Adventurer standing beside him, his eyes glued to the action that they can see.

The battle rages on for another thirty minutes then peters out as the drums change. Bugle calls bring the Adventurers back to their original position as the Champion strides back to the command post, shaking blood off his sword. A quick shake of his head negates the question asked of him while all around, soldiers and healers work to deal with the toils of combat.

Time drags on, runners moving between the supply wagon and the front to provide drink and replacement equipment. A command is given, and within the circle of wagons a series of cook fires are started. Without warning, the drums begin again, though the cooks in the centre ignore it all, working on their task.

Daniel finds his stomach rumbling, hunger risen from the constant state of excitement he has been in. He can do nothing, see nothing, just guess at what is happening, yet his excitement will not decrease, nervous energy draining and energising him at the same time.

The battle this time seems to go much the same to start with, but after ten short minutes, a human roar begins. The line at the back, at first orderly, suddenly breaks apart in the centre and then spreads outwards quickly, the army disappearing past the hill in pursuit. The Adventurers quickly break up into hunting groups, tasked with dealing with the flanks even as the commanders take leave, following along behind the army themselves.

For a time, silence reigns on the battlefield and Daniel looks to Maximillian, unsure if that was it. So much time for so little gain. Even before he can open his mouth, a low growl from Asin makes him look at her. She points, and he follows her finger, following its path across the road to where a group of Orcs reveals themselves from amidst an untouched copse of trees.

Chapter 28

There is not much time to say anything as the Orcs, realising they are spotted start off at a run to the group. Cries of alarm resound around Daniel, and he does not realise his voice has been added to the throng.

Mia and Kilroy turn themselves to face the oncoming horde, other Adventuring parties streaming up to reinforce the line from behind them. They are on the far right of the too-thin line, and Daniel can feel his mouth go dry as he sees the lumbering enemy. The Orcs are clad in a variety of clothing ranging from filthy rags to battered leather armour, though a pair of massive Orcs behind are clad in full chainmail. Outside of their clothing choices, Daniel is unable to spot differences in the screaming green, tusk-filled, hatred spewing creatures that bear down on him.

Mia begins firing first along with a few of the other competent archers, sending their arrows into the horde. A few falter, arrows catching them in shoulder, chest and leg but most other shots miss. It is only a short moment later, and another twenty meters before the crossbowmen among the group start firing, adding their bolts to the deluge. Kilroy does not even look, handing over his crossbow to Daniel who passes him his own before beginning to load Kilroy's. Daniel forces himself to stay precise, ensuring that he gets the bolt seated properly before he begins cocking it. The moment he is done, he hands the crossbow over and notices how close the Orcs are.

How did they get so close? Daniel thinks, surprised as he drops the crossbow Kilroy passed to him and grabbing his shield and mace to join the battle. The melee fighters like Maximillian have already taken off, charging the larger group to ensure they are not bowled over. However, the line is too thin, and Orcs swirl around the Adventurers, rushing the line behind them.

Having barely had time to set himself, the Orc facing Daniel almost bowls him over entirely from the initial rush. Daniel staggers back and only the sudden push from behind as Kilroy throws his shoulder into the younger man helps him keep his feet. Thankfully for Daniel, the Orc is unready for the burst of electricity that arcs through him from contact and Daniel is able to duck beneath the mistimed strike. He brings his own mace into play, smashing the Orc in the face twice before booting the creature away from him.

Above the fighting, Asin is working her throwing daggers into the rushing horde, catching Orcs in the feet and face and causing them to falter in their headlong rush. The initial rush stalled, she begins to target her throws with care, picking on Orcs that attempt to flank and gang-up on nearby Adventurers.

Mia and Kilroy, having dropped their ranged weapons have drawn a sword and a pair of knives respectively and work next to Daniel as he pushes forward, using his Shield Bash ability to create space for them to attack. In the centre of the fighting, the Adventurers have fallen into a quick circle to back each other up and avoid being surrounded entirely. Maximillian still stands, wielding his sword and dagger combination expertly, catching and turning aside blows with his dagger and striking back with the sword in quick, precise movements.

Daniel continues to push forward, instinct driving him to close to his party member and help him. A blow to his left is caught on his shield, Kilroy taking the opportunity to slip in behind the Orc's attack to drive his daggers into the Orc's chest. Daniel brings his own mace down in a crushing blow on another Orc facing Mia who is forced to abort its own attack to dodge the strike, giving Mia a moment to recover her footing. As the Orc steadies itself after the dodge, a thrown dagger drives through its throat, piercing it completely through. Distracted and choking on its own blood, Mia ends the creature's life.

A loud roar catches Daniel's attention just as he finishes engaging Double Strike, smashing the next Orc in line before him aside. Both of the massive Orc Warriors that Daniel first spotted have joined the fray in the centre, smashing aside the flimsy circle through brute force. Maximillian spins away from an attack against him, blade flicking upwards to slice tendons in the arm as he faces one Orc Warrior. The second Warrior rampages through the remains of the line.

Distracted for a brief moment, Daniel is almost struck by the Orc facing him, only a last-minute jerk of his head stopping the blow from braining him. It lands against his shoulder though, numbing his left arm for a moment. Daniel growls, ducking forwards and closing with the Orc to give himself a moment, punching the creature in the face with his mace in hand. When the Orc backs away, he backhands the creature and then shoves it to the right to allow Mia to finish the creature off.

Maximillian dances away from the large Orc Warrior, the creatures wide, inexperienced swings giving Maximillian brief breathing room as other Orcs are forced to scramble away to ensure they too are not hit. He uses the time to launch his own attacks, striking arms and legs when he can. As the Orc grows angry, it steps forward to end the fight, and that is when Maximillian steps forward in a perfect lunge, his sword glowing briefly and punching through the chainmail. The impaled Orc Warrior finishes its initial attack, though the weakened blow is easily turned aside by Maximillian's dagger.

Unfortunately, before Maximillian can retrieve his sword from the Orc Warrior's body, the other Orc Warrior returns, swinging his sword at Maximillian. It catches the Adventurer under his chest but is unable to pierce the plate breastplate the man wears. Still, the blow is strong enough to lift the Adventurer off the ground and throw him several feet away.

Kilroy roars, pushing away from the group to become a blur of flickering blades as he whirls through the last few remaining Orcs between him and his party leader. The blows leave long, bleeding gashes on all his opponents, drawing their attention to the dagger-wielding fighter in their midst. As they concentrate on him, Daniel and Mia rush them from behind, laying waste to the distracted fighters.

Behind, Asin has jumped down from her wagon and is working her way among the remaining Adventurers, killing their opponents with quick strikes of her daggers from behind before pulling them into a cohesive unit. Unknown to Daniel and his focused friends, they have pushed deep into the main group and created a flanking manoeuvre by themselves, and Asin works to finish rolling up the Orcs with the others.

Daniel finally closes in on Kilroy and Maximillian. A Shield Bash pushes one last remaining Orc off Kilroy, who is bleeding from multiple wounds already but refusing to move away from his downed party leader. Spotting a brief moment of respite, Daniel drops his knee and places a hand on Maximillian's prone body to cast Minor Healing. The casting takes precious seconds but is quicker than his Gift and less dangerous to use in such circumstances. Above him, Mia and Kilroy fight aggressively to keep the Orcs off Daniel to give him time to work.

As Daniel looks up from casting the spell, he is greeted by the sight of Mia's sword being driven aside as she mistimes her block and is overwhelmed by the sheer strength of the remaining Orc Warrior. The blow enters her left shoulder blade, shearing through muscle and bone and leaves her stunned and bleeding. Daniel surges to his feet, triggering a Shield Bash into the Orc Warriors mid-section, though it is Daniel who is sent stumbling backwards. The Orc Warrior is not deterred from his attack, swinging its sword again at Mia. Daniel throws himself in the way, bracing his shield with his other hand and staggering back. He keeps staggering as the Orc Warrior does not relent, swinging blow after blow at Daniel, never letting him set himself properly, each blow widening cracks across the shield.

The relentless attacks of the Orc are suddenly halted as a pair of throwing knives sink into its deltoids as Asin and her collected Adventurers finally arrive. Asin herself moves to flank the creature, throwing her knife with Piercing Shot to distract the creature further as Daniel charges ahead with his Double Strike. Working together, the two Adventurers fall into the routine they have developed to deal with Ogres on the seventh floor, whittling the more powerful Orc Warrior down with each blow. Beside them, the other Adventurers work to finish mopping up the remaining Orcs, leaving the two to finish the job.

In contrast to the desperate battle only a few moments ago, the battle with the Orc Warrior now is almost too easy. Injured beforehand, and with no other distractions to bother them, the Orc Warrior is no match for the two rookie Adventurers. When the Warrior collapses from Daniel's final blow to its forehead, the two adventurers step aside to look for further danger and find none. The battle for the supplies is done.

Chapter 29

For a brief moment, Daniel relaxes, relief flooding through him that he survived the carnage. A moment later, he sheaths his mace and shield as he rushes over to Mia's body. Her wound is wide open, blood no longer pouring from it, and even as he bends down to check, he knows it is too late. Still, he tries but the soul has fled, and his Gift finds nothing to purchase upon.

Grief threatens to overwhelm him but is pushed aside as Daniel moves to do his job. Kilroy limps over, tears running down his cheeks as he stares at his friend's body. The grieving Adventurer goes to one knee, holding her as sobs rip themselves from his chest.

Only Asin sees this, for Daniel works feverishly, moving from body to body to do what he can. Other Adventurers work to triage the situation, pulling the grievously injured aside while Daniel and the other healers stabilise them. Daniel uses his Gift sparingly, only doing so twice to quickly heal and stabilise Adventurers that would otherwise expire. Those that are injured but who will survive are cared for with more traditional means, mana saved for all but the most critical.

It is only when the critical work of healing is done that Daniel is able to check the notifications that have been piling up, scanning through the various pieces of information he has received during the fight. It is only the last piece that is of particularly noteworthy.

Level Up!
Adventurer Level 5
You have gained 5 attribute points.

When the first army division returns and no other attacks come, the healers turn back to their patients, using their mana to speed up the healing process. All efforts are taken to conserve some mana for potential additional life-threatening injuries, but with the immediate danger over, the healers have wider leeway to use their spells.

Maximillian is among those critically injured but stable, ribs shattered but the internal bleeding halted by Daniel's quick fix. Daniel himself works on his wounds, using his healing skills to patch the unconscious party leader together. Kilroy has been pulled away by now from Mia's body, and he sits next to Maximillian, clutching the departed Adventurer's bow as he watches Daniel work.

Asin works with the quartermasters while Daniel heals, first stripping the Orcs of their valuables and then categorising it all. A part of the Catkin is disappointed that the Army will be taking it all, but she accepts it without complaint. This is neither the time nor place to discuss the terms of their hiring after all. In either case, it is a better task than the distasteful one of burying the Orcs and her peers.

It is in the evening that the Champion finally reappears with the rest of the Army. Tents staked and perimeters secure, the party begins. Losses were more than acceptable; the Army once mobilised had managed to destroy the grunt Orcs with ease. Only once was there true danger when the Orc War Chief himself had joined the battle, but the Champion had met him in combat himself. The tale of the Unbreakable defence of the Champion's Gift and the ensuing fight travelled the tents with speed, growing with each telling.

Those guarding the supplies have their own tale to tell, and while the celebration is at first muted, it soon picks up. The Adventurers understand loss, they understand death, and while this was not the way they expected their friends to go, it was still part of their job. Grieving could happen, would happen, later – for now, it was time to celebrate the fact that they were alive.

In their own camp, Daniel and Asin find themselves in a cook-off much to the delight of surrounding camps. The two cooks have beer pressed into their hands while they work to feed the hungry crowds, laughter and good-natured ribbing passing between them. Or as much ribbing as Asin ever offers.

In the morning, the camp breaks up, and the Army begins its long journey home. A select few of the Adventurer parties do not go back, instead moving to the border to ensure that the Orcs are gone. Daniel and his group are not chosen, their group too few and new to take part in such an endeavour. Daniel is relieved – as instructive as this quest has been, he is happy to return home.

The journey back to the city is quiet and relaxed, even the Army personnel seeming to loosen up after the battle. Daniel spends his time alternating between the healers' wagons and walking alongside Asin to start learning Catkin.

At the city gates, Daniel never makes it all the way to the Adventurer's Guild to file his completed Quest. Instead, he is dragged away firmly by Khy'ra to celebrate his safe return. After the throes of passion, she expertly drags the tale out of him, letting him work through his emotions. Asin completes the Quest for both of them, giving Liev a quick hug before departing to see her family. In their own way, the Beastkin debrief her, making her tell the tale of the battle again and again to different groups. It is only the next morning that Daniel manages to make it to the Adventurer's Guild, lighter of step with a portion of his grief eased.

"Daniel, good. I have something for you," Liev smiles slightly, waving him over.

"Morning, Liev. Asin let me know." He nods to his friend, looking around the relatively quiet Adventuring Guild. It seems most of the others who went with the army are taking a day off.

"Come with me," Liev beckons and brings Daniel to a private room. There, he pulls a small packet out of his jacket pocket, offering it to Daniel. When opened, it contains a simple iron ring with a cut blue-purplish stone. Yet, when Daniel picks it up, he gets a notification:

Moonstone Ring of Experience
On sleeping, wearer re-experiences events occurring within 24 hours, learning new lessons.
Effect: +2% experience and skill gain over previous 24 hours

"This…" Daniel's jaw drops. He has heard of enchanted items like this before of course, stories told by Adventurer to Adventurer, their status raised to almost mythic proportions. Enchanted items like these were passed on as heirlooms in Adventuring families, guarded as some of the most precious items they could acquire. It was said the Crown itself was made of Moonstone, granting the wearer a 10% boost. To hold a ring like this in his hand exceeds his expectation.

"It's yours. I would caution about speaking about it to anyone else. Khy'ra, of course, knows as she negotiated it as your payment for the healing of the Champion," Liev says. He reaches out, closing Daniel's hand over the ring.

Daniel fights his feelings, truly conflicted. His first, instinctive reaction is to refuse the gift. It is too much, way too much. Yet, a more honest part of him realises how powerful and appropriate a gift it is – letting him gain strength and experience even as he loses it while using his own Gift. It could never truly make up the ground lost or the memories forsook, but it would help.

"Thank you." Head bowed, Daniel opens his hand and slides the ring on.

"No need. I'm just the messenger." Liev smiles, patting the young adventurer on the shoulder and guiding him out.

Outside, Asin waits patiently with a slip in her hand. She glances at Daniel and Liev and sees the new ring but ignores its presence, instead proffering the quest slip to Daniel. Daniel smiles at his friend, taking the slip and reading it over before raising an eyebrow. "Shadow Cat, again?"

Asin nods firmly, caressing her knives. Their one failed quest. For a moment, Daniel hesitates then he smiles, acceding to her request and walking to the counter. "Back to work it is then."

###

Author's Note

If you enjoyed reading the book, please do leave a review and rating. Not only is it a big ego boost, it also helps sales and convinces me to write more in the series!

If you enjoyed this, check out my other series:
- Life in the North (An Apocalyptic LitRPG)
https://readerlinks.com/l/729295
- A Gamer's Wish (An Urban Fantasy LitRPG)
https://readerlinks.com/l/729151
- A Thousand Li (a cultivation series inspired by Chinese wuxia and xianxia novels)
https://readerlinks.com/l/729231

For more great information about LitRPG series, check out the Facebook groups:
- Gamelit Society
https://www.facebook.com/groups/LitRPGsociety/
- LitRPG Books
https://www.facebook.com/groups/LitRPG.books/

About the Author

Tao Wong is an avid fantasy and sci-fi reader who spends his time working and writing in the North of Canada. He's spent way too many years doing martial arts of many forms and having broken himself too often, now spends his time writing about fantasy worlds.

If you'd like to support him directly, Tao now has a Patreon page where previews of all his new books can be found!
https://www.patreon.com/taowong

For updates on the series and the author's other books (and special one-shot stories), please visit his website: http://www.mylifemytao.com

Subscribers to Tao's mailing list will receive exclusive access to short stories in the Thousand Li and System Apocalypse universes:
https://www.subscribepage.com/taowong

Or visit his Facebook Page:
https://www.facebook.com/taowongauthor

About the Publisher

Starlit Publishing is wholly owned and operated by Tao Wong. It is a science fiction and fantasy publisher focused on the LitRPG & cultivation genres. Their focus is on promoting new, upcoming authors in the genre whose writing challenges the existing stereotypes while giving a rip-roaring good read.

For more information on Starlit Publishing, visit our website!
https://www.starlitpublishing.com/

You can also join Starlit Publishing's mailing list to learn of new, exciting authors and book releases.
https://starlitpublishing.com/newsletter-signup/

Read an excerpt of Book 2 of Adventures on Brad series:

An Adventurer's Heart

Chapter 1

As the sun begins to set, a pair of Adventurers approach the Northern city gates of Karlak. The small dungeon town is bisected by a river, overlooked by rolling hills, and surrounded by wooden walls. The town radiates outwards from its chief income source, a Beginner Dungeon with buildings closest to the Dungeon and the town center made of stone, and those further away with cheaper materials such as wood and clay. As the pair near the walls, the Guards relax as the pair are well known, and their presence barely missed. After all, these two Adventurers had left only two days ago.

The taller of the pair is only five-foot-eight, a friendly smile gracing his face as he nods to the guards. The friendly Adventurer is broad and stocky, his muscular frame currently burdened by a large bag slung over his shoulder. The second of the two is a shorter Catkin female, black fur and bestial, cat features on a slim build. She is dressed in a jerkin and shirt, with a dirty, once dark-blue coat trailing behind her. A brace of throwing daggers lie across her torso, another larger pair rest on her hips as she glides alongside her partner.

"Matthew, Jason!" the human Adventurer calls out, waving in greeting as he shifts the bag behind him again.

"Daniel, Asin. A successful trip I take it?" The two guards grin, glancing at the bag and the roll of dark fur that lies strapped to the top of it.

"Yes!" Daniel answers them, pride radiating in his voice.

"Well, best get in. We'll be closing the gates soon." The two guards beckon the Adventurers into the town, and Daniel nods in thanks. Asin chuffs a greeting as well, the guards flashing a quick, narrowed eye once-over at the Beastkin before stepping aside.

When the pair is a distance away, Asin moves closer to her friend, grating out in a low purr, "They like you. The guards."

Daniel nods, smiling slightly as he rubs his nose as it attempts to get used to the unwashed, rotting stink of the city, "Yeah. They're a decent lot mostly."

Asin chuffs again, shaking her head at Daniel but failing to contradict him directly. His experience and hers differed greatly as the Beastkin were an unwanted, barely tolerated minority in Brad still. If she had arrived alone, Asin knew she'd have to pay the toll for coming in and would have been hassled for leaving, even though she was a registered Adventurer like him. Daniel, however, had managed to build a good reputation in the town – his work in the Clinic as a free healer and his time spent socializing with the guards stood him in good stead. His presence shielded her and those with him, even if he himself never realized it.

The pair head deeper into the town, bypassing alleys that would take them into the various shopping districts and head directly to the Adventurer's Guild. The Guild is one of the few buildings in town able to afford the mana stones required to light the building all night long and does so, staying open all hours of the day and night. They could afford this as the Guild was the exclusive purchaser of mana stones from the Adventurers who ventured into the Dungeon, their monopoly guaranteed by Kingdom law. It is also at the Guild that the two expect to turn in their successful quest.

It is no surprise to either of the Adventurers to find that Liev, the red-haired senior Guild attendant, is still on duty. He rarely leaves the building and is often seen working the busy shifts late into the night when Adventurers returned from their Dungeon exploration. When the pair step into the building, Liev smiles as he spots them, straightening up for a moment from his usual slouched posture before the usual impassive demeanor returns.

"Asin, Daniel. Back already?" he says to them when the duo finally reach his window.

"Yes!" Daniel unslings his bag and unties the skin, dropping it on the counter as proof of their successful hunt.

A brief check is all that Liev requires to confirm the kill, and then he hands over their reward, a staggering 75 silver, and their deposit. A single silver could let a day laborer who skimped eat for a year, so the sum they have just earned still makes both Asin and Daniel grin. After all, it has only been a bare nine months since they first started Adventuring. The enormous sum for the Quest was due to the continued failures by other Adventurers to complete the quest. As was custom, the city raised the bounty after each failure, using a portion of the failed Adventurers lost deposit to pay for the increase.

A brief moment later and both Adventurers receive a notification, the glowing black lines floating in their sight before disappearing.

Quest Complete!
+5,000 XP

The pair of Adventurers quickly take their piles of coin, thanking Liev before exiting to run their next errand. Asin leads Daniel to a butcher shop, having organized the additional trade to supplement their income. Shadow Cat meat was a rare treat and would be highly sought after by certain clientele, and the butcher had agreed to pay very well. Once again, Asin chuffs in pleasure at the thought of the coin they are about to earn and the fact that her party member had done most of the hard work carrying the meat back to town. In truth, while the work had been hard,

Daniel knew the additional funds would help in paying off their accumulated debts.

Absently, Asin strokes the matching enchanted bracers on her arms. While they had greatly aided the pair in their battles, enchanted weaponry was extremely expensive and had driven both of them deeply into debt. Even now, with their recent windfall, they would have been unable to pay for the bracers if Tharuk, the enchanter, had not generously agreed to allow them to pay what they could, when they could. For Asin though, owing anyone, especially a Dwarf, was not something that sat well with her.

Meat deposited and payment received, the two Adventurers part ways. Asin to meet her family and Daniel to head to the Spinning Top, the inn where he resides. At the inn, Daniel greets Elise the innkeeper and owner before asking for food to be brought to his room, taking the time to wash himself down in the provided washbasin. After dinner, exhausted from a hard day's work, Daniel lies back on the clean sheets and falls asleep, completely forgetting about the dinner he had ordered.

***

As he sleeps, his enchanted ring of experience begins to draw forth the stored memories from its stone, replaying them through his mind and body in flashes. It is a strange experience as the memories and experiences that flow through his mind are always somewhat scattered.

In the morning, Asin is cooking breakfast, spreading herbs on the omelet and working the pan with little flicks of her hand. Mushrooms, field onions and more.

"Ugh, no mushrooms!" Daniel complains and Asin sniffs, ignoring his constant complaints about the delectable fungus. "I'll cook mine!"

Daniel takes over when Asin is done. Borrowing the pan, he cracks the eggs with professional ease. Instead of borrowing from her herbs though, he pulls his own out from his pack, separating each pouch and adding in the herbs with practiced flicks. Asin sniffs as she watches, though an eyebrow arches at his last addition.

"Papricha," Asin grates out.

"Yes, paprika. Love it," Daniel smirks and finishes up, tossing the omelet onto his plate and pulling out some bread to toast as well. "Want some?"

Asin pauses, nose wrinkling and whiskers trembling in the still air before she bobs her head, tail lazily waving behind her.

The Shadow Cat is crouched above Daniel, snarling at the downed Adventurer. He groans, pushing against the monster but it's already jumping away as Daniel tries to lever the monster off him, blood pooling on the ground from the cat's attack. A knife catches the Shadow Cat as it jumps away, Asin's Piercing Shot drilling into the creature's body, the knife twisting as it rotates in. Attached to the knife is a long iron chain, the end of which is wrapped around Asin's torso.

The creature's jump pulls the chain taut, jerking it to a stop and forcing the monster to fall with an ungainly crash. Asin, who is lighter, is pulled off her feet and falls on her behind. The snarls of pain and dismay from the pair of cats sound eerily similar to Daniel as he struggles to his feet.

Standing, Daniel jumps at the monster, slamming the mace down with his full strength onto the cat's prone form. He clips the creature's back leg, bruising and tearing muscle as the cat attempts to stand again. Asin rolls over, gripping the chain and yanking hard to throw the cat off balance and keeping it out of the shadows.

Daniel swings again, the blow catching the cat on its forehead, dazing the creature and then he kicks it away from the nearest shadows to the middle of the path they walk on. As he does, the knife finally dislodges, and Asin stumbles from the sudden release. She catches herself quickly enough to pull another knife to throw at the cat, even as the monster gets back onto its feet in another attempt to flee.

Walking back to the city, back bowed as he carries the quartered meat. Daniel asks, "Where did you learn to skin and butcher like that?"

"Father. Traditional," Asin chuffs, waving a hand around and then goes back to cleaning her claws, working to remove the accumulated blood and filth.

"Ah," Daniel nods slightly, a wry twist of the lips crossing his face. He never knew his father, a casualty of the mines a few years after he was born. His mother had died in childbirth, leaving him to grow up with his grandfather. Strange how that still stung, even after all these years.

Morning. The bells wake Daniel up and he pulls himself from the covers, drenched in sweat once again. He sighs, shaking his head at the memories and unpleasant experiences he has gone through. Sometimes, it seemed that the minor gains in experience he received from the stones were not worth the hassle.

Continue reading here:
https://readerlinks.com/l/729349